A WILD GHOST CHASE

A REAPER WITCH MYSTERY

ELLE ADAMS

This book was written, produced and edited in the UK, where some spelling, grammar and word usage will vary from US English.

To be notified when Elle Adams's next book is released, sign up to her author newsletter.

The day after I got fired from my job at the morgue, I woke to the sound of a ghost turning on my computer.

"Hey, you've got mail." Mart hovered above my desk, reading something on my laptop screen.

I groaned and covered my head with a pillow. "I thought I told you to leave my laptop alone. If it's another message from my old boss, I don't want to know."

I'd assumed taking a job at the local morgue would be right up my alley, relatively speaking, but I don't know why I'd thought dealing with dead bodies for a living would make their ghosts less likely to cause trouble for me.

The pillow floated into the air and threw itself at my face. I batted it away, and it flew around and hit the back of my head. Scowling, I pushed the bedcovers aside. "Not necessary, Mart."

"I beg to differ." The pillow thumped me on the skull

again. "I could do this all day. Sending a picture of you sleeping to your ex in three, two, one…"

"Don't you dare!" I flew across the room and slapped Mart's transparent hands away from the laptop.

The day my twin brother had figured out how to operate a computer from beyond the grave had marked the end of my brief aspirations to work in an office. In the regular world, most people didn't automatically jump to the conclusion that a ghost was responsible for messing with their computers, but after a week of my co-workers' mouse icons moving by themselves and inappropriate videos randomly playing during important presentations, I'd decided an office job wasn't for me *or* the ghost who shared my apartment.

As I'd found out yesterday, the morgue wasn't much better.

I took over the keyboard and deleted a swathe of emails in case Mart got it into his head to start sending pictures of me sleeping to potential employers instead. I never should have let him figure out how to use my phone camera, that's all I'm saying. When you've been dead for eight years, you get bored easily. Eight years is longer than most spirits tended to stick around, but he was stubborn like that. It ran in the family.

I scrolled through my emails. "Junk, junk… another rejection, a request for a CV from a magical recruitment firm… no thanks."

"You need money." Mart stuck his hand through my shoulder from behind, sending a shiver running through my whole body as though someone had just waltzed over my grave. I really hated when he did that. "You didn't get on with a regular job, so maybe you should suck it up and go back to the magical world."

"I'd have got on better with regular jobs if I didn't have an annoying ghost for a flatmate," I pointed out. "Ghosts don't need to pay bills, so you don't get to give me career advice, either. Also, I should at least be charging you for using up all my hot water."

For reasons I couldn't fathom, Mart liked turning on the shower and standing underneath the water. He claimed it made him feel alive again. Since nobody else could see or interact with him, I let him have his small amusements, but I did not need the extra water bills at the moment. In fact, I was a month away from getting kicked out of my apartment unless I managed to scrape together enough money to pay the next rent instalment.

Maybe he had a point that the magical world was more fitting for me, but to date, I'd fared even worse in magical careers than I had in normal ones. After all, the normal world just thought I was a little odd. The magical world, on the other hand? Let's just say that in certain circles, I'm considered a troublemaker at best, dangerous at worst.

I deleted yet another email. "Most of these positions are too far away."

"You can fly," Mart pointed out. "So can I."

I shook my head. "I just settled here. Okay, it's a bit of a dump, but it's the best I could get for one person."

Sharing a house was out of the question with my ghostly companion, but my job history did not make me an impressive prospect for most landlords. Add in the issues Mart had caused for my previous neighbours and it was a wonder I'd found someone willing to rent to me at all. I was pretty sure the only reason I'd been offered this apartment was because the previous resident had been a criminal who'd taken off without paying any bills, and even a live-in ghost was less unappealing to the landlord. Marginally.

"A bit?" he said. "The dripping tap keeps me awake and I don't even need to sleep."

"You just like complaining." I closed my inbox. "Nothing worth getting up for in here."

"Then what's that notification?" He waved a ghostly hand at the screen, where an icon had popped up in the corner.

"An old email address," I said. "I didn't apply for any jobs using that one, so it'll be junk."

To placate Mart, I opened my old inbox and came across an email sitting in the junk folder, addressed to 'Reaper Witch'.

Hi,

You don't know me, but I need to hire someone to get rid of a ghost and I'm told you're the best. I'd really appreciate it if you came to help me out.

Thank you,

Carey Forbes.

PS - I can pay.

At the bottom, she'd put her address as somewhere in a town called Hawkwood Hollow. I'd never been there before, which was one point in its favour. Most magical places I'd lived in wouldn't have invited me back even if I'd promised them a free exorcism. My ghostly sidekick was only one of the problems I brought with me wherever I went.

"Do it," Mart said. "It's easy money. You can banish a

ghost with both hands tied behind your back."

I drummed my fingers on the desk. "This Hawkwood Hollow… have you heard of it?"

"Nope," he said. "If we finally found a magical town you haven't alienated, you should head there right away."

I gave him a scowl. "It's not me who usually does the alienating. Not on purpose, anyway."

Mart was right, though. I needed money, fast, and the odds of finding a new position before my next rent bill was due were low. And while I'd hung up my metaphorical scythe years ago, the fact remained that the best way to make a bit of quick cash was for me to make use of my one dependable skill. This wouldn't be the first time I'd broken my personal rules to take care of a little ghostly problem for someone—which explained why this Carey person knew my old nickname. Reaper Witch.

"All right." I closed my laptop and got to my feet. "I'll go and get rid of this ghost."

If nothing else, it would be a welcome break from the monotony of job applications and interviews, trial shifts and dead ends. The morgue incident hadn't been entirely my fault, but it was kind of hard to explain to ordinary people that their loved one's ghost had been following me around for days, requesting changes to his own funeral plan. After a solid week of pestering, I'd finally agreed to contact his family in order to get him to leave me alone.

Needless to say, it hadn't ended well.

This Carey Forbes had already heard of my reputation as a ghost hunter, so with luck, the people of Hawkwood Hollow wouldn't be too surprised when I showed up. If they hadn't already found someone to get rid of this ghost, then perhaps there wasn't a local Reaper who could take care of the problem. Officially, each magical community was supposed to have at least one Reaper, but some places got skipped over for whatever reason. Which was good news for me, because a town without a Reaper meant fewer awkward questions.

Namely, the question of who had broken the Reapers' all-important rule against interbreeding with humans. Not that anyone would dare ask that question to an actual Reaper. Most people had a healthy fear of asking the local Angel of Death about their love life, after all.

First, I had to actually *find* Hawkwood Hollow, which meant inputting the address into my witching location app and hoping for the best. Most magical towns were isolated, while paranormal communities were usually protected by spells which rendered them invisible on any regular map and prevented ordinary people from wandering in. A necessity, because most magical folk are about as subtle as a troupe of unicycle-riding clowns juggling fireballs.

I opened the app on my phone screen to reveal a route straight from here to Hawkwood Hollow. "Just need to fly north."

"I'm looking forward to this." Mart flew beside me as I left the flat and locked the door behind me. "It's no fun when you're the only living person who can see me."

I did the usual check to make sure nobody was close enough to hear me talking to myself. "I thought you enjoyed the attention."

A fair proportion of witches and wizards could see ghosts, so he'd have no shortage of people to give him the attention he wanted in Hawkwood Hollow. I drew my wand and cast a camouflage spell on myself before retrieving my broomstick from underneath the porch. Then I swung one leg over the side and took off, fixing the image of the route in my mind. The cloaking spell ensured nobody in the streets below looked up and saw me flying over the rooftops and into the cloudy sky.

"Why're you still using a broomstick?" Mart asked. "I think you should invest in a pair of Seven-League Boots. Much more efficient."

"They got banned, in case you've forgotten." I steered the broom against the wind current coming in the opposite direction. "The last witch who used those boots took one step too far north and ended up in the Arctic Circle."

Mart cackled with laughter. "I'd pay to see you do that."

"If you could pay, I'd charge you rent." I held my broomstick in a firm grip as the wind battered at me. "Besides, if I freeze to death, there'd be nothing anchoring you here."

"You can't freeze to death." He spread his arms wide. "Reapers can't die from exposure."

"Not keen on testing that theory." I pressed myself flat against my broomstick as he swooped overhead, making noises like the TARDIS from *Doctor Who*. "Can you stop fooling around? How old are you?"

"Technically, I'm still older than you are," he replied.

"But you're still as mature as a ten-year-old." In actual years, he was the same age as me, but he was forever stuck at eighteen and didn't act a day older than his death. Didn't look it, either. While we both shared the same curly dark hair, mine bounced to my shoulders and tangled in knots when the wind currents pinned me to the back of my broomstick. We'd once had the same blue eyes, too, though ghosts' eyes faded out and mine remained as bright as a typical Reaper's. My eyesight was better than average, but I still had to duck lower than the clouds to keep an eye out for the right town.

After Mart had got bored of chasing pigeons around, he flew in behind me until we touched down on a grassy expanse in the middle of nowhere. A river bisected the field, and a large number of houses popped up out of nothingness as the wards which kept the town hidden recognised the presence of a paranormal visitor.

I dismounted my broomstick, transported it back home with a flick of my wand, and walked downhill towards the town. Magical communities varied as widely as their inhabitants and I half-expected to be accosted by a security guard demanding to know who I was and what I was doing here. Nobody stood waiting, however, so I walked downhill and onto the dirt track leading into the town, checking the address on my phone again. Even from the ground, a thin layer of fog hung over the buildings. Hawkwood Hollow? *Haunted* Hollow was a more appropriate name.

"I don't like this place," Mart announced.

"What do you mean, you don't like it?" I frowned at his transparent figure. "You're a ghost. You're adaptable."

"It's cold."

"So is the afterlife." It *was* cold, though. I hadn't thought to wear thick layers, so I drew my wand and cast a quick warmth spell. Heat spread from my toes to my fingertips, and the two of us, one dead and one living, walked on towards the cluster of houses on the river.

A chill mist swept around us, almost masking Mart from sight. It'd be hard to spot any other ghosts in here, but my plan was simple: walk into town, find the ghost, and get rid of it. Zero drama, zero distractions, and zero trouble from dead people.

Okay. Almost zero. There was no getting rid of Mart—and I should know, considering I'm the only person I know who *could* get rid of him if I wanted to.

I stopped at a crossroads, using my phone to check the address Carey had given me. The houses seemed to be arranged at complete random, with the numbers running in all directions along crooked lanes spreading outwards from the river like a spiderweb. The buildings themselves ranged from newly built to hundreds of years old. I took three wrong turnings before returning to the river. *This is ridiculous.*

As I was debating finding someone to ask for directions, a transparent figure floated past over the bridge.

"Hey." I walked behind the ghost. "Excuse me?"

The ghostly man wheeled around on the spot. "You can see me?"

"Well, yes." Maybe he wasn't the ghost I'd been told to banish. With most troublemaking spirits, there tended to be more screaming involved than polite conversation. "I'm looking for Mrs Renner's house."

"That way." He pointed, then leaned closer to the glowing tip of my wand. "Oh… you're warm. I can almost feel it…"

"Big mistake there," Mart snickered, while the ghost hovered closer as though hoping to leach some warmth from my living body.

I ignored both of them and walked in the direction the new ghost had pointed me in, past the river and towards a row of detached houses arranged as though someone had pulled random numbers out of a hat. Number five, fifteen, seventy-five… seriously? Who'd designed this place?

Mart blew on the back of my neck. "Hey, Maura."

"Not now, Mart."

"Maura."

"I said, not now." I looked up from my phone screen, annoyed. "Stop badgering me."

Mart cleared his throat. "You might want to look behind you."

Despite myself, I rotated on the spot and squinted into the gloom. Two more ghosts had joined the first, drawn by the light and warmth of my wand. "Shoo." I waved a hand at them. "Go and haunt someone else."

I was far from the only witch with the ability to see ghosts, but apparently, nobody else living was out on the streets today. I turned my back, only to see three other ghosts approaching from the opposite direction. *What in the world is going on?*

Mart gave a low whistle. "Wow."

"What?" I looked where he pointed. Then my jaw dropped.

A large number of flickering phantoms filled my field of vision. Adults and children, witches and shifters and countless others.

This was bad. This was really bad.

The entire town was swarming with ghosts.

2

"Let's get out of here." I turned away, but there was no ghost-free escape route within sight. Worse, all the spirits had seen me looking at them, and the warmth spell was too much for them to resist.

Of course, that would change when they realised that I was a Reaper who could banish them straight into the afterlife if need be. Most spirits who stuck around longer than a day got a little attached to their continued existence, however insubstantial, and were utterly terrified of anyone who might put an end to it. Mart was an exception, but he'd known me while he was still alive, after all, and he'd rather do almost anything than admit to being terrified of his twin sister.

I walked on down the foggy street, thoroughly spooked for possibly the first time in my life. Were there no living people in this town? The email I'd got from Carey hadn't indicated the town was uninhabited, but it sure looked that way to me. This was officially the creepiest town I'd ever been in—and for a Reaper, that's saying a lot.

I rounded a corner and found the entire road blocked by ghosts. That was the last straw. I might not carry a scythe like an official Reaper, but I could improvise if I wanted to. In an instant, shadows crept around my feet and surrounded me like a shroud. Then I put on a deep, sinister voice, "Leave, now."

The ghosts fled, every last one of them. Some cried, "Reaper!" as they flew away. Others just vanished into thin air or swarmed away from me, dispersing throughout the town.

Only Mart remained behind, shaking his head at me. "Was that really necessary?"

"I was asked to banish *one* ghost," I told him. "If I hadn't got rid of the spares, I'd never be able to get the job done."

"You just wanted an excuse to bring out the dramatics," he said.

"If you want to believe that, it's fine." In truth, I wished I'd just stayed in bed. Hawkwood Hollow was a literal ghost town in the worst sense possible. Either some horrible magical plague had killed off the population, or they had generations of ghosts hiding among the living without anyone being inclined to do anything about it. The latter option was more likely, but you'd think the local witches who had the ability to see ghosts would have staged a mutiny by now. Or hired an actual Reaper.

Maybe this was the true reason why this Carey person had invited me here, and she'd conveniently forgotten to mention that there was more than one ghost in town. More like a hundred.

I spotted someone on the bridge heading towards me. *Finally, a living person.* She was maybe fifteen or sixteen at most, though her outfit made her look younger—a school uniform in shades of white and mustard yellow, bright red socks patterned with broomsticks, and a pair of red goggles perched atop her head.

The girl bounded up to me. "Are you the Reaper Witch?"

"Call me Maura," I said. "Are you the person who emailed me?"

Had she seen the ghosts flocking around me? If she was a witch herself, then she might be able to see them. I couldn't imagine Hawkwood Hollow would be a pleasant place to live for anyone who had the ability to see ghosts —which generally, was about a third of the total number of witches and a hundred percent of the Reapers.

"I am, yes." She rocked back on her heels. "I didn't know who else to ask to help. I'm Carey."

"Shouldn't you be at school?" The question escaped before I could consider keeping my mouth shut. But I'd come here specifically to *avoid* trouble, and witch academies could be pretty hardcore when it came to truancy.

She lowered her gaze. "Um, yeah. I took a day off, because the ghost is particularly active this week and I need the footage for my blog."

"Blog?"

"Yep." With every step, those goggles of hers bounced on her nose.

"What are you wearing?" I asked.

"Ghost goggles. They make it easier to see spirits." She looked up at me. "Are you really her? The Reaper Witch?"

How in the world had she heard of me? Okay, there

was that time I'd agreed to be a guest on a popular witching show a few years ago, *Hannah's Hauntings*. I was pretty sure about five people had watched that episode, so it was a little bewildering that anyone might actually remember it.

"Just call me Maura," I said. "You run… a ghost blog?"

"Yes," she said. "Not a very popular one, though. Not yet. I have three subscribers. But when they find out I have the Reaper Witch here to help me, they'll tell all their friends, I'm sure. We'll go viral."

We? No thanks. I did not need any publicity. Even the most obscure blog might draw the sort of attention I'd prefer not to deal with if I could help it. Namely, the Reaper Council.

"I'm not sure you'd like that," I said delicately. "I've never been in a town this haunted before, and to be honest, I'm not all that keen on being followed by ghosts everywhere. I'm going to deal with that spirit of yours, as I promised, but then I have to run back home."

"Hey!" Mart said indignantly. "Not keen on ghosts? What am I, then?"

"But—you came all this way," she said, without so much as a glance in Mart's direction. "My mum runs the Riverside Inn, so we have plenty of space. You're welcome to stay as long as you need to."

It came as a surprise to hear the town had any tourism at all. "That's nice, but really… I can stay an hour or two, but no more."

It seemed in bad taste to mention I needed the payment, but if I didn't find a way to pay this month's rent, I'd end up spending next month camping in a field. I had exactly one marketable skill, as the universe seemed determined to remind me. A warm room sounded like heaven, I wouldn't lie, but I hadn't planned to wind up in a town with more ghosts than living people. The sheer number of lost spirits pointed to a problem far deeper than any single haunting. A problem which would require more than one ex-Reaper to handle.

"Oh," she said in a small voice. "Okay."

"I didn't mean I'm not happy to be invited here," I added, with a twinge of guilt. "Honestly, I'm surprised anyone even remembers that interview."

"I've watched it so many times I can recite it from memory," she announced. "I've been a fan of *Hannah's Hauntings* since the beginning. I especially liked the episode with the haunted toaster."

Oh, boy. "Is this haunted house nearby?"

"This way." Carey turned on the spot, skipping along as though we were going to Disneyland and not a haunted house. Her goggles wobbled on her head, while I followed more slowly, my second thoughts multiplying.

"C'mon." Mart nudged me from behind, sending a wave of ice-cold down my arm. "It'll be fun. I've always wanted to stay in a haunted inn."

"You're usually the one doing the haunting," I whispered. "I'd have thought you'd want to leave more than I do, in case the other ghosts steal the spotlight from you."

"Nobody can replace me," he said. "I'm unique."

"Weren't you just telling me you didn't like the look of the place?" I hissed. "Now, be quiet, before she realises I'm speaking to a ghost and wants to look at you through her ghost goggles."

Given that she hadn't already spotted Mart, I figured her ghost goggles could use some fine-tuning. She didn't seem to have noticed the other ghosts, either. While I'd frightened them off earlier, some of them were already starting to creep back into view at the edges of the streets.

A ghost, a blogger and a Reaper Witch walked into a haunted house. It sounded like the start of a bad joke. I just hoped it wouldn't end like one.

"Who's the ghost, then?" I caught up with Carey. "If I know her name and what she looks like, it'll be easier for me to identify her."

Carey slowed her pace. "The ghost is a local woman who lived alone. This is her house."

She indicated a large Victorian detached house which sat alone on the riverbank behind a rusty gate and a low garden wall of crumbling stone. The door was painted red, though faded, while the whitewashed walls were battered with wear and tear. One of the downstairs windows was boarded up, and another had cracks spider-webbing across the glass. Despite the air of neglect about the place, however, the house itself was practically the size of a mansion. Way too big for a single person.

"Whoa," I said. "The ghost lived here?"

"*I* want to live here," Mart declared, jumping over the wall and marching straight through the closed door. Serve him right if he got sucker-punched by a ghost.

"Mrs Renner has lived in that house for decades," explained Carey. "The place was in the middle of being renovated when she died, so it's a bit worse for wear. Unfortunately, anyone who's tried to fix up the place since has been driven off."

"Oh, so that's why you need me to get rid of her," I surmised. "I'm guessing it's difficult to sell a house with a screaming ghost in it."

She nodded, her goggles bouncing on her forehead. "Yeah, she's been causing trouble for the renovators all week, so I thought I'd hire someone to take care of the problem. No witch or wizard has been able to get rid of her."

"Okay." Now we were speaking my language. "I'll need to talk to the ghost before I can figure out how to proceed. Should we head inside?"

"Sure." She pushed open the gate and fiddled with the ghost goggles, hitting a button on the side. "I'll just turn the microphone on."

"Turn the *what* on?" I was starting to wish I'd just gone into the house alone instead of consulting with her first.

"Are you coming in here or not?" Mart called out.

I ignored him. So did Carey... which suggested she *couldn't* hear ghosts. If our unwanted spirit accosted us inside the house, I'd have to handle her alone. Nothing new to me, but the house seemed empty of both living and dead aside from Mart, while my long-dormant Reaper senses didn't detect anything waiting on the other side of the door. The old woman's ghost must be hiding deep inside the house.

As Carey gave the goggles another shake, I cleared my throat. "I don't know if you've ever tried recording a ghost before, but they don't tend to show up on camera."

"I know." She pulled down the goggles, revealing lenses so thick and dark it was a wonder she could see through them. "That's why I have these. They're fitted with spirit lenses which can detect ghosts."

"Can you actually see anything else through them, though?" I asked dubiously.

"Not really, but I only have to put them on when

there's a ghost in my line of sight." She pulled them up onto her forehead again.

I could think of at least a dozen problems with that theory, but I decided not to burst her bubble. Yet. "Do you run the blog by yourself?"

"I do," she said. "This is the first time I've been near an actual ghost, so I need to get as much footage as possible."

I cast my mind around, but I couldn't for the life of me find a polite way to tell her to give up the goggles and let me handle everything else. Ghosts had a tendency to mess with technology, and besides, I didn't want her camera to record me in action if I had to pull out all the stops to get rid of the ghost. The living weren't supposed to witness a Reaper's work. Even an unofficial one like me.

Carey adjusted her goggles and pushed the gate open with a loud creaking noise. Then, she said, in a dramatic whisper, "And here we are, entering the abandoned house of Mrs Renner, who tragically died last week when a door frame collapsed on top of her."

"Wait, that's how she died?" I asked, momentarily forgetting every word I said was being recorded. "Was it an accident?"

"Good question." Her voice dropped to a whisper again. "Her death appeared to be a tragic accident, but the rumours circulating the town of Hawkwood Hollow say otherwise. Only her ghost can tell the truth."

"Carey, you do realise your recording device won't pick up a sound from a ghost, don't you?" I said. "Only us."

"This one is different." She tapped the side of the goggles. "It picks up on sound waves, and it should work equally well on the dead as the living."

"Have you used it on a ghost before, then?"

"No, because I haven't been allowed into the house," she said. "They just removed the police tape this morning."

I halted, halfway through the gate. "So we're breaking and entering."

"It's not breaking and entering when nobody lives in the house," she said. "Is it?"

Magical laws were not my strong point. "Technically, her ghost lives in the house, so she's within her rights to throw us out."

For all I knew, the magical law enforcement would have an issue with us being here, too. Yet the absence of anyone on the streets suggested nobody was keeping a close watch on the place.

Her brow furrowed. "What? She's dead, though. The dead don't have rights."

"I wouldn't say that where she might hear you." I dropped my voice, glancing over my shoulder in case anyone had seen us enter the garden. "Ghosts can be a little... territorial. And sensitive. They don't like being reminded they're dead."

"Even when you're banishing them?" she said, now looking thoroughly confused.

"Banishment is usually a last resort," I told her. "I try to reason with each ghost first to convince them to leave of their own accord, before using that option. So we have to treat her like she's still one of the living and then try to persuade her to leave. If that doesn't work..."

If that didn't work, then the scythe came out. Not that I had one of those anymore, and I most definitely would *not* be carrying out a banishment with a teenage girl as my audience. Even if she couldn't see ghosts, she could see *me,* and Reapers were as terrifying to the living as they were to the dead. Or so I'd been told, anyway.

"The house is mine now," Mart called out from behind the door. "You can't come in."

Honestly. It seemed he hadn't found the house's other ghostly inhabitant yet, at least.

"Who was she, then?" I asked Carey. "Mrs Renner, I mean. Did she have any family? Anyone who's likely to be irked at us for breaking in?"

"No family here in Hawkwood Hollow," she said. "She didn't leave a will behind, so nobody knows who's going to get the house. Anyway, I don't think it counts as breaking in. Nobody's been here since the police left."

"Did the police think her death might not have been an accident?" I asked.

She shrugged one shoulder. "I don't know. I mean, I know they questioned everyone who was at her house recently and didn't draw any conclusions, so I assume they gave it up."

Hmm. One major reason a lot of ghosts stuck around after death was due to unfinished business... like an unsolved murder. But I'd have to take up that line of inquiry with the ghost herself.

"If you don't have a key, how were you planning to get in?" I scanned the front of the house.

"I do have a key." She reached into her pocket and whipped out a jagged metal shape with triumph. "It's homemade. Fits every lock. Well, it should. I haven't tried it yet."

Oh, boy.

My doubts continued to multiply as I crossed the garden to the doorstep. If Carey failed to get us in, I could use that as an excuse to leave, but something about this situation struck me as suspicious in multiple ways. A ghost, a dropped murder case and a lack of a will left behind equalled trouble in my book.

And that wasn't even getting into the sheer volume of ghosts here in Hawkwood Hollow. It wasn't natural, even in a magical community. But I couldn't think of a subtle way to ask if the town had suffered some horrible tragedy in the past. From what I'd seen of the ghosts, they'd ranged from old to new, from elderly pensioners to the occasional child or teenager. There was no pattern to it whatsoever.

There came a click as she turned the key in the door, which swung inward. "It worked?"

"Yes, it did." Carey beamed and put the key back in her pocket. Then she tapped on the goggles again. "We're about to enter the abandoned house, where Maura the Reaper Witch is about to have a showdown with a ghost. Who will be the victor?"

Me, I hope. I'd never met a ghost I couldn't banish… and with luck, the spirit would bring some answers about what was really going on in this town.

3

Despite its size, the house was as dilapidated on the inside as it was on the outside. The wall-paper peeled off in strips, revealing the brick beneath, while patches of carpet dotted the stairs on our left-hand-side. On our right was a living room, containing nothing except a grand piano coated in dust... and Mart, hovering above it. He waved furiously, but I paid him no attention. I'd rather not have to explain to Carey that another ghost had already entered the house.

"She died here." Carey pointed to a doorway in the middle of the hall, separating one half of the house from the other. "Can you see her ghost?"

"No ghosts here." *Except my brother.* "If I start talking to myself, that's usually a sign one of them has come after me."

"Maura is the ghost whisperer," she said into the microphone. "Her unique ability to communicate with spirits is second to none."

Mart cracked up in silent laughter. I gave him a glare,

smoothing out my expression as Carey frowned at me. "Something wrong?"

"I don't think we should raise our voices in here," I said. "Just in case. What exactly did the witnesses say the ghost did to scare them off?"

"Huh?" She blinked. "I heard she kept slamming the doors, mostly, and someone said they heard screaming."

"I'm trying to gauge how strong she is," I said. "The most powerful ghosts can move objects around, turn lights on and off, things like that. Screaming is annoying, but fairly harmless."

"Hear that?" She lifted the ghost goggles, raising her voice. "Maura claims the most powerful ghosts can affect the physical world. Join us as we uncover the secrets of Mrs Renner, whose mysterious death has baffled residents of Hawkwood Hollow. How powerful might she be?"

Mart snorted. "Hey, if that thing works on ghosts, can it hear every word I say?"

I didn't respond, but Mart began to sing at the top of his voice. I mimed elbowing him in the spine and a flood of icy cold swamped my entire arm.

"Cut it out," I hissed out of the corner of my mouth.

"Some ghost goggles those are." Mart flew behind Carey, blowing on the back of her head. I suppressed a sigh. He was determined to make a nuisance of himself, it seemed, and I found myself fervently hoping that Carey's recording device *didn't* turn out to work on the dead.

I walked up to the curving wooden staircase, which rounded a corner to the upper floor. "Might she be hiding upstairs?"

"Maybe." Carey adjusted her goggles, seemingly oblivious to Mart's attempts to get her attention. "How do you usually do your ghost-hunting? Do you have equipment or anything?"

She looked me over as though wondering if I had a bunch of ghost-hunting gear hidden underneath my coat. If I were a real Reaper, I'd be carrying a scythe, but most people wouldn't be able to see it. Still, I didn't need one to get rid of a spirit. I just needed to know where it was hiding.

"It depends on the ghost," I replied. "Some of them want attention and don't need much encouragement to come out. Some like hiding and playing tricks on people. Some are open to negotiation, while others only respond to force."

"Negotiation?" Her brow furrowed. "How does that work? You tell the ghost why they should leave the house?"

"In theory," I said. "Doesn't always work, but it's generally worth trying. With the stronger ghosts, once you start telling them to leave, they can get… violent."

"Oh." She looked down, biting her lip. "But you're an experienced ghost hunter who can handle anything?"

"Pretty much," I said. "But I think I should probably speak to the ghost alone. Sometimes they don't like being cornered."

"I won't get in your way," she said. "Besides, someone has to record the whole experience, don't they? Otherwise, I won't have anything to upload to my blog."

"I'm not sure the ghost will like that either."

Mart floated up and stuck his head through Carey's face. "I'd love to be a guest on your show."

Carey startled, shaking her head so hard the goggles

nearly fell off. "Did you feel that? It went really cold. I think the ghost might be here."

Nah, it's just my annoying brother. "I don't see her. Anyway, I think we should check upstairs first."

I directed that comment at Mart, who could float up through the ceiling and see if there was anyone upstairs without either of us needing to follow. Given the state of the cracked plaster on the ceiling, I was a little concerned it might collapse if I trod too hard on it.

Mart, however, ignored my implied request. Carey pushed up her goggles and spoke into the microphone: "And now, having completed our inspection of the lower floor of the house, our only option is to head to the upper floor in search of our elusive ghost."

By the time we reached the upper floor, I was seriously considering sneakily using my wand to throw the recording device out the window and then blaming it on the ghost. If the spirit was as angry as Carey claimed, she wouldn't take kindly to being treated like a novelty, and the last thing I wanted was to accidentally get the two of us on the hit list of a vengeful spirit. Then I'd have zero chance of leaving Hawkwood Hollow without causing a huge scene and potentially endangering Carey's life. Besides, thanks to Mart's antics, most of the recordings would end up being worthless at this rate.

I stepped onto the landing, where the floorboards creaked alarmingly underneath my feet. I squinted through the doors to either side, seeing each room was in as much of a state of disrepair as the ones below us. "Carey, is there a light switch?"

"Yes, but it'll ruin the atmosphere," she whispered back. "Besides, the ghost might be hiding."

"I'm not sure she's even here." I peered into each room, finding nothing but dust and ancient wooden furniture. I was retreating back to the stairs when there came a creaking sound from somewhere on the lower floor.

"Is someone down there?" I called.

No reply. That was promising… or not. What if someone else had caught us in here? A living person, that is? We *were* technically trespassing, and we'd seen no signs of the ghost whatsoever. Mart had gone awfully quiet, too. I assumed he'd got bored and drifted off elsewhere, but the lack of any ghosts upstairs seemed suspicious after the number of spirits I'd seen outside. *Where is this ghost?*

A loud yell came from downstairs. *Mart.*

"Are you okay?" I called back, but no response came.

Nothing frightened Mart. Nobody could see him… except for other ghosts.

"Who, me?" said Carey. "Wait, did you hear her? Mrs Renner's ghost, I mean?"

"No." *Mart.* I trod back towards the stairs, and the front door blew open. A tremendous blast of wind roared through the house, slamming into me like a train. I caught the wall for balance, and a rattling whisper came out of the air.

"Stay away," hissed the voice.

Carey whimpered and gripped my arm, her nails digging into my skin. "I heard that," she whispered. "Was that the ghost?"

I dipped my head in a faint nod and trod downstairs towards the open door, holding onto the banister with my free hand. The wind picked up speed, and a clanking noise made me jump. It took me a panicked instant before

I realised Carey's goggles had fallen off and bounced downstairs into the hallway.

I reached the foot of the stairs and picked them up, my nerves jangling, and looked upright to see a tall, fearsome figure leaning over me.

I yelped and jumped to my feet, holding the goggles in front of me like a shield—then lowered my hands when I realised I wasn't looking at a ghost at all. The man, very much alive, was six-foot-something and broad-shouldered with longish dark hair and an expression of utter disbelief on his face.

"What are you doing in here?" he demanded. "This is private property, and the scene of an ongoing paranormal investigation."

"It doesn't look like one." My tone came out more belligerent than I'd planned, but my heart was still beating a million miles a minute and my body still thought we were being chased by velociraptors. "What paranormal investigation?"

"Mine," he responded. "My name is Detective Drew Gardener, and I'm here investigating the death of Mrs Elizabeth Renner. This house is off-limits until my say-so."

"It's my fault." Carey stepped out from behind me. "I hired her to come here to get rid of the ghost."

"I'm a sort of unofficial ghost hunter," I added. "I was told there's a spirit here which is proving difficult to remove. I didn't know there was an active investigation on."

"I'm sorry." Carey hung her head. "I was only trying to help."

The detective regarded her with a mixture of exasperation and sympathy. "I understand that you feel a sense of responsibility since you're the one who found her body, but bringing an amateur ghost hunter from out of town isn't going to help the situation."

Carey found the body?

"Amateur, am I?" I folded my arms. "Did you see who blew the door open just then? Did you hear her voice?"

"I heard it," Carey said. "I heard the ghost tell us to get out."

The detective shot her a sideways look, then turned back to me. "Think you're being funny by terrorising a teenage girl, do you?"

"Excuse me?" I said. "Did you seriously not hear anything? You should at least have seen the door open by itself."

"Gust of wind," Drew said, as though that settled the matter. "Nothing more."

"Uh, no. You have a ghost in here." I glanced up at the ceiling. "A pretty strong one. Carey tells me all the renovators who've tried to work in here have been frightened off."

"Wizards are easily spooked," he said.

"If they can see and hear ghosts, then of course they are," I said. "You, however... I don't know what *you* are."

His brow cocked. "Why not guess?"

Er... not a wizard. He must be paranormal, though I couldn't tell what type. A warning voice in the back of my head told me I wouldn't do myself any favours by making him angry, but he was the one who'd refused to accept the ghost's presence here. One of us was in denial, and it wasn't me.

"A sceptic," I said. "Who can't see ghosts."

"It sounds like the only person here who claims to be able to see ghosts is you," he observed. "Care to tell me whereabouts Mrs Renner is?"

I caught Mart's eye over his shoulder. *Good. He's okay.* "Nope, but there's another ghost behind you right now."

"There is?" Carey grabbed for her goggles. "Where?"

Typically, Mart chose that moment to retreat from view. As Carey looked up and down, I caught sight of the detective's sceptical expression. Now I thought about it, I didn't want to explain my dead twin brother to this obnoxious stranger.

"Never mind," I said. "It's clear some people only believe the evidence of their own five senses."

He grunted. "I don't see anything wrong with that."

"When you're dealing with a house you can't sell because there's a ghost living in it, then you have a problem," I pointed out. "I'm sure the renovators wouldn't like to hear you're implying they're lying, either."

"You're not from Hawkwood Hollow, are you?" he said. "It's none of your business. What's it to you if Mrs Renner's house gets sold or not?"

"I get paid if I get rid of her, for a start." I sensed Carey's eyes on me. "Also, if everyone here believes the same as you do, it'd explain why you have enough ghosts here to start a haunted theme park."

Carey gasped. "I *knew* it! I knew we were swimming in ghosts. I just need to fine-tune my equipment better."

The detective frowned. "You shouldn't play along with her like that. It's manipulative."

"Who are you, her parent?" I said. "You think I flew all this way to prank a teenage girl? If you don't want to believe this house is haunted, that's your prerogative, but unless you want a visit from a Reaper, I'd suggest you start taking the ghost situation seriously."

"A Reaper?" he said. "We have one. We don't need another."

"Wait, there *is* a local Reaper?" I arched a brow. "Slacking off on duty, isn't he?"

"What do you mean by that?" he said.

"Hello?" I gestured to the town in general. "I'm pretty sure the dead outnumber the living in Hawkwood Hollow. You're only the second living person I've seen since I came here."

"Don't be absurd," he said. "You've been here, what, an hour? Yet you still feel the need to make sweeping statements?"

"I *saw* them," I said. "And I assume a fair few of your citizens can, too. So what is your Reaper playing at?"

His eyes narrowed. "I thought you were here to deal with a ghost, not make judgements about a magical community you don't belong to. And I don't see you making any effort with the former, despite your supposed talent."

"Excuse me?" I glanced at Carey, unable to believe the cheek of this total stranger. "The ghost in question took off when you came galumphing in here."

A muscle ticked in his jaw. "If you make as much noise as you did while you were coming downstairs, I rather think you're more likely to have driven her away yourself. Though I'm more inclined to believe you're making excuses."

"Right, and the door blew itself open." Now I remembered why I spent more time hanging around the dead than the living. Even ghosts weren't usually this infuriating.

"This is a creaky old house that's practically falling to pieces," he said, undeterred. "It's not my concern if there's a ghost here or not. I'm here to ascertain the nature of Mrs Renner's death, no more. Now, leave."

He had some nerve ordering me around. He couldn't even see the ghost, not if he wasn't a wizard, so he had no business assuming he was the only person who had a chance of finding out if the old woman's death had been an accident or not.

"I take it your investigation doesn't involve speaking to the woman herself?" I queried. "Because if I can find her ghost, then I can ask who killed her. Seems more efficient than your method."

"That's not for you to say," he said. "I'm going to ask you once again to leave this house. If you don't, I'll have to call the authorities to remove you."

Well, that was uncalled for. "I was under the impression you *were* the authority. Or do you make a habit of ordering around everyone you run into?"

Carey grabbed my elbow. "We should go. C'mon."

She all but ran out of the house, while I turned and raised an eyebrow at the detective. "Terrorising teenage girls, am I?"

Before he could respond, I exited the house myself in case he really did decide to call the police. Lucky he couldn't see Mart hovering behind him, making rude gestures. *He thinks he can call the shots, does he?* Serve him right if the ghost decided to haunt *him* instead of the house.

Haunted or not, we'd have zero chance of coaxing out

the house's deceased inhabitant with Detective Grump wandering around. He strode out of the house as we reached the gate, probably to ensure we didn't sneak back in. As he did, Mart flew right through the detective's body, and he halted, a frown on his face, but he didn't otherwise react to my dead brother's presence.

"What a piece of work," I muttered to Carey, opening the creaky old gate. "Is he the reason you can't get anyone else to get rid of the ghost? I doubt it helps matters that he doesn't even believe in them."

"Well… the ghost hasn't actually been seen, just heard," she said. "I hoped you'd be able to draw her out."

"I might have been able to, had our esteemed detective not decided to butt in." I pulled up my hood as a few drops of rain fell. "Great. Looks like I'm going to be flying home in the rain."

"You're leaving?" A hint of disappointment underlaid her voice.

"I just got thrown out of Mrs Renner's house." I tried to keep my tone kind. "It's clear I'm not welcome here."

"You'll be welcome at the Riverside Inn," she insisted. "My mum was looking forward to meeting you."

"She was?" Were her entire family fans of that one obscure interview I'd done on *Hannah's Hauntings* years ago? It seemed unlikely.

"You're famous," Mart said from behind my shoulder. "I hope you make a better impression on her than you did on that snooty guy back there."

I ignored him. The raindrops became more frequent, and before long, rivulets of water ran off my coat. Why had I decided flying here was a good idea? The perils of mixing broomsticks and thunderstorms filled a whole section in the magical health and safety rulebook. If the local authorities were as pedantic as that detective, they'd probably tie my broomstick to the ground as soon as I tried to take off.

Thunder rumbled in the sky overhead. "Wonderful."

"Come with me," said Carey. "My family's inn has a restaurant and bar, and both are open until late evening."

A bar sounded like a good idea to me. I needed a stiff drink to wash away the lingering annoyance from my encounter with the detective and the guilt over failing to track down the ghost.

Besides, as reluctant as I was to fall back on ghost-hunting as my main income source, nobody insulted my spirit-banishing abilities and got away with it. Ghosts were my area of expertise, and thanks to that meddling detective, I now had an extra incentive to figure out what was going on with this particular wayward spirit.

On the other hand, I had nothing with me but the clothes on my back, and they were in danger of being totally soaked through. I'd check out the town's inn and speak to Carey's mother before I decided on my next move.

The Riverside Inn sat on the other side of the stone bridge arching over the river, resembling a family-run bed and breakfast with a neighbouring restaurant connected to the inn via a pair of automatic doors in the reception area. Inside the restaurant, witches, wizards and shifters mingled with goblins and elves and other magic folk, chatting and eating.

Oh, and then there were the ghosts, of course. I counted only four of them inside the restaurant, fewer than I'd seen elsewhere in town, but they all looked curiously in my direction as we walked in. From the looks we drew from the patrons, too, I gathered strangers weren't a common sight here in Hawkwood Hollow.

The young witch behind the counter, who had a blond pixie cut and several piercings, put down the glass she was polishing. "Hey, Carey. Got the day off again?"

"Yeah." Carey looked down, her face flushing. I'd been wondering how her family would feel about her skipping school, but the girl behind the counter looked too young to be her mother. "This is Maura, by the way."

"Hey," I said awkwardly, conscious of the number of stares levelled in our direction from both the dead and the living. "Don't you get many visitors from out of town?"

"Not that many, but the restaurant is popular," said the girl. "I'm Hayley. Are you staying next door?"

"She is," Carey put in, before I could reply. "Maura's here to help with Mrs Renner's ghost."

I suppressed a groan when several people in the vicinity glanced our way, with double the curiosity this time.

The girl behind the counter arched a brow. "Oh? Really?"

"Actually, we didn't have much luck earlier," I said. "Seems our ghost is a little shy."

Hayley picked up the glass and resumed polishing. "Can you see ghosts, then? I heard it's rare."

"Depends whereabouts you live," I said. "I'm guessing it must be rare here, or there'd be more complaints." I glanced at the four ghosts hovering around in the corner, all of whom busied themselves talking to one another when they saw me looking.

"There are ghosts in here?" Carey pulled down her

goggles so hard they fell off and bounced on the floor. She ducked down and picked them up with a sheepish expression.

"You know… forget I just said that," I said.

The nearest wizard was looking at me as though he thought I was a few cards short of a deck. Carey, too. This situation was precisely why I didn't mention my abilities to most people, even witches, yet the number of ghosts here in Hawkwood Hollow was on a whole other level. Someone had to have noticed.

"Wow," said the girl behind the counter. "I can see why Carey wanted to hire you. What did you do, put out an ad in the paper?"

"She did an interview once," Carey said. "It was on *Hannah's Hauntings.*"

"Oh, you're famous?" Her eyes sharpened with interest.

"No," I said quickly. "It was a one-time thing, years ago, and… never mind. I think I should—"

"Carey?" a voice said from behind me.

She spun around, her eyes brightening. "Oh, hey, Mum. This is the Reaper Witch."

If everyone in the restaurant hadn't already thought I was an oddity, they definitely did now. The woman in front of me looked like an older version of Carey, minus the school uniform. Her long brown hair was streaked with grey, while she wore a vibrant red cloak and a matching pair of spectacles balanced on the end of her nose. Her socks were also red, patterned with broomsticks like Carey's.

"Just call me Maura," I said. "It's nice to meet you."

"I'm Allie Forbes." She stuck out her hand for me to

shake. "Carey told me everything about you. She showed me the interview, too."

"She did?" I'd honestly forgotten what I'd even said in that interview. It was years ago, back when I'd thought I might still be able to make a go of this ghost-hunting thing. Several near-miss situations with the Reaper Council had since crushed that notion. I shook her hand quickly and reached for an excuse to get out.

"She said we have some ghosts here in the restaurant," Carey told her mother.

"We do?" Allie's gaze flickered around the tables. "Not dangerous ones?"

"Nah, they're fine," I said. "Ready to move on, I'd say. I'm surprised the Reaper hasn't seen to their departure."

"Oh." She gave a brief glance at the patrons, who'd gone back to their meals as though they weren't listening in on our conversation. "There hasn't really been an official Reaper here for a while… our last one retired without a replacement."

"Meaning he's turned his back on us," said a nearby wizard in a carrying whisper.

So the Reaper was well-known, then? If not for the rain, I might have taken the opportunity to go looking for him. Granted, I was more tempted to take the detective's advice and get out of here while I had the chance, but there was no way I'd let a rude stranger dictate my life choices. I needed the money, and whatever Carey's mum said, this town seemed lacking in a Reaper to clean things up in the ghost department. I was kind of surprised the Reaper Council hadn't already paid a visit, given the state of the place. The ghosts didn't look like they were suffering in torment or badgering the residents, for the most part, but they also shouldn't be hanging around a family restaurant. At least it seemed most of the guests couldn't see their ghostly visitors.

Some of the tension left me when a few people walked up to the bar to order drinks, taking some of the attention off us.

"Is that true?" I asked Carey's mother in a low voice. "Who is the Reaper, anyway?"

"Old Harold isn't known for being social," she said. "Reclusive, you know… I haven't seen him in years. Anyway, what happened with Mrs Renner? Did you see her ghost?"

"No, but I did hear her." I glanced around, but since everyone had returned to their own conversations, I didn't think they were eavesdropping any longer. "She yelled at us to get out."

Her brows shot up. "That's why you left?"

"No," I said. "Not because of her, anyway. Some guy calling himself Detective Drew Gardener booted us out because he said we were trespassing on a crime scene."

"What absolute nonsense," she said. "There's no open investigation—not an official one, anyway. Of course there's gossip about the old woman's death not being an accident… poor Carey had to deal with some nasty comments about that, but that's more due to the unfortunate circumstances than anything else."

I frowned. "What does that mean?"

Carey winced. "I found the body, so… some of the other kids at the academy started spreading rumours around."

"Right, the detective said you found Mrs Renner," I recalled. "What happened?"

"I heard a crash inside the house when I was walking past," she mumbled. "So I knocked on the door, and it wasn't locked or properly shut. I saw her lying in the hallway, and I called the police. I swear I had nothing to do with it."

I had to admit it was very unlikely that she'd done anything to hurt the old woman. Besides, who was I to blame her for keeping that little piece of information a secret? I had enough skeletons in my closet to throw a party in there.

"I believe you," I said, "but if her death wasn't an accident and there *is* an investigation going on, I don't want to step on any toes."

Especially if they belonged to an annoying so-called paranormal investigator.

"I'll tell the detective we hired you, and that should take care of the problem," said Allie. "Carey, dear, will you go and tell Hayley to get Maura a drink? What would you like?"

I glanced over my shoulder. The rain wasn't clearing up, and besides, it wouldn't hurt to stick around here and hope Careys mother could shed more light on the town's history. I'd already made a mental note to pay a visit to the Reaper.

"I'll have a coke, please." I'd save the heavy drinking until later. If I was going to visit a reclusive Reaper who'd been neglecting his duty for years, I'd need it.

4

I hadn't intended to stay in the restaurant all afternoon, but the rain didn't let up until early evening. Carey still seemed to be under the impression I'd be staying more than a day, which I'd really prefer to avoid—even if the idea of flying on a broomstick in the dark was as unappealing as the idea of flying in a heavy thunderstorm.

Allie was a talker, it turned out, and within two hours, I knew everything there was to know about the hotel and the restaurant, not to mention the tourism issues the town had been having over the last few years. While she didn't directly blame the ghosts, I was pretty sure they had something to do with the high levels of mist hanging over the rooftops and the general atmosphere of gloominess. The inn and restaurant had few permanent staff, which meant Carey helped out most weekends and after school. Allie insisted she head off to do her homework in the early evening, while I went to look out the window and found the rain had finally stopped.

I headed over to Carey's mother. "Allie, whereabouts did you say the local Reaper lived?"

"He lives in a small cottage next to the graveyard," she said. "That's down the road from the local witch academy. You can't miss it. Are you sure you want to visit him, though? He doesn't like strangers."

"I'll be honest with you," I said. "This town has a rampant ghost problem. I've never seen anything like it before. It's not just about Mrs Renner—though I can ask him about her, too, and see if I can get any answers on why she stuck around."

"It's up to you," said Allie. "I wouldn't advise you to bother him unless there's no other choice, but who knows, maybe he'll be willing to talk to you."

That didn't sound promising, but the Reaper ought to have the authority over Drew the paranormal investigator who didn't believe in ghosts. It was about time I found out how a Reaper had let the town become completely overrun by spirits. This wasn't the result of a few weeks of neglect, but a few years at least. Pretty much unheard of in a magical community.

"All right," I said. "I'll be back later."

When I left the restaurant, I saw ghostly figures drifting up and down the streets, mingling with the living people crossing the bridge over the river and heading home from school or work. Some of them might as well have been dead for longer than I'd been alive. Allie had already told me she'd raised Carey more or less single-handedly after the death of her husband a decade ago, as well as running the hotel, but I hadn't asked if his ghost was among the town's inhabitants.

Frankly, I didn't even know where to begin with the

ghosts, so my best bet was to check in with the person whose job revolved around them. More than a job. Reaping is a life calling, and one did not turn one's back on it without consequences. Even someone like me, half witch and half Reaper, with no ties to the Council.

I crossed the bridge and turned down the street, following Allie's directions.

"Hey!" Mart caught me up, huffing indignantly. "You never asked if I was okay after my frightening experience in old Mrs Renner's house."

I slowed down to let him catch up. "Did you see her ghost? Is that why you yelled?"

"No, of course not," he said. "I heard that detective stomping around and thought I was done for."

I snorted. "I doubt it was that traumatising for you. He doesn't even believe you exist."

"How dare he?" His arms folded across his chest. "Thanks for the existential crisis. It's going to keep me up all night, that is."

"You don't sleep anyway." I walked on, hands in my pockets. "Anyway, you're going to have to hide when I see the Reaper."

"Oh, you're finally doing something useful?" Mart said. "I thought you were going to sit around chatting all day."

"It was raining, and that detective kicked us out the house," I reminded him. "Besides, you don't need to ride a broomstick in the rain to get home."

"I'm tied to wherever you are, in case you've forgotten," he said in sullen tones. "I'm stuck in this town as long as you are."

"But you can still explore," I pointed out. "Which I'm

assuming is what you were doing while I was talking to Carey and her mum. Find any interesting ghosts?"

He shrugged. "None as interesting as I am. Say, is that your new friend?"

I spotted Detective Drew ahead of me and took a sharp turn to the right to avoid him. "He'd better not be visiting the Reaper, too."

"Not if he doesn't believe in ghosts."

"Weirdo." I buried my hands in my pockets. While I'd got a few more ideas of how the town had come to be in this state—most regions had at least one permanent Reaper assigned, if not more—I was no closer to understanding why Detective Drew had claimed to be running an official investigation into Mrs Renner's death. Not that I wanted another conversation with him, so I carried on my way.

My detour added a good ten minutes to my walk, but I was glad of it when I reached the local cemetery and found it blissfully detective-free. A small brick cottage at the foot of the hill was numbered 42. There were no other houses on the road at all, so I assumed the numbering was just another local quirk. That, or a joke.

"Is that a Hitchhiker's Guide to the Galaxy reference?" Mart peered at the number on the door.

"Ask the Reaper." I walked up to the cottage door and knocked.

"Go away!" yelled a voice from inside.

I squinted through the blurred glass window, but I couldn't see who spoke to me. "I'm here to talk to the Reaper."

"The Reaper is retired," he responded.

"Not if there's no replacement."

The door flew open. A scowling grey-haired man stood in the doorway, his eyes startlingly blue. Reapers might look human, but most regular people would describe our eyes as otherworldly. Or terrifying. No wonder some people called us the Angels of Death. Luckily, I got most of my genes from my mother's side, and not every Reaper would recognise me as one of them right off. From his scowl, he hadn't figured it out yet.

"What's it to you?" he said. "Why've you come to disturb me?"

"I'm here to talk to you," I told him. "I'm Maura, and I'm visiting Hawkwood Hollow to help deal with a troublesome spirit."

"Visiting, are you?" He halted beside a tall coat rack from which a long dark cloak hung. Wait, that wasn't a coat rack... that was a *scythe* he'd hung his coat from. If ever I'd needed proof that he'd hung up his Reaper coat, that was it.

"May I come in?" I pressed.

"Fine, fine." He backed into the doorway, affording me a closer view of the menacing curved tool he'd hung his coat and hat on. I'd never seen a Reaper use their most powerful Reaping tool as a piece of furniture before. Then again, this guy called the shots in the area.

The inside of the cottage left a lot to be desired, too. Dirty carpets held years of grime and a thick layer of dust covered the furniture, as though it hadn't been cleaned in a very long time, if ever. I wondered how long ago he'd retired and left the town to end up mired in ghosts. If there'd been no major disasters in recent times, then it must have been at least a decade. No wonder the place was overrun. No ghosts lurked inside his house, though it would be simple for him to get rid of them.

I cleared my throat. "So, you may have noticed there's a lot of ghosts around here."

He grunted. "Tell me something I don't know."

Right. It seemed he was well aware of the problem. Which he would be, if he was one of the few residents who could actually see them. "Did you hear about old Mrs Renner? She died recently, and her ghost is being disruptive to everyone who tries to go into her house and renovate the place."

He backed into a cluttered living room, sat down in an armchair with half the stuffing spilling out, and lit up a cigarette. The smell of smoke infiltrated the hall and I stifled a cough.

"So, I'm looking for an explanation as to why she won't leave," I added, in case he hadn't got my meaning.

"Ask her, not me," he said. "I haven't been near the place."

"I've heard her death might not have been an accident," I went on. "Is there a procedure for removing angry ghosts? Or do you always hire people from outside?"

Like Detective Drew, for instance?

"As I told you—" He exhaled in a puff of smoke, making my eyes water—"I haven't been near the place. If you've seen her ghost, then ask her what she's sticking around for. Not me."

His attitude was starting to grate on my nerves. "I haven't seen her ghost. I *have* heard her yelling, and our esteemed paranormal investigator refuses to believe she's there. I came to you because of all the people in town, I assume you *can* see and deal with stubborn spirits who won't leave after death. Given the scythe in your hallway, it's clear I came to the right place. Why haven't you offered to help out?"

"I'm retired," he grunted. "No more Reaping for me."

"Didn't you have an apprentice to take over from you?" I asked.

"No!" He removed his cigarette from his mouth and threw it at me. I ducked on instinct, and it hit the door frame, fizzling out on contact.

"Hey!" I backed into the hallway. "I'm not here to usurp your position, but this town will end up on the list of the regional Reaper Council if you don't deal with some of those ghosts. It's your job, and your duty."

Oh, great. Now I sounded exactly like my father.

"Who are you to lecture me about duty, you posh little witchling?" He picked up another cigarette. "Get out of my house."

Shadows flooded the room, spreading outward from his feet. His eyes glowed brighter, while the room darkened by the second. While he wasn't a tall or imposing man, there was something forbidding about him which hadn't been there before, despite the lack of a scythe in his hand.

I summoned up my own shadows in retaliation. I didn't even have to think about it. Darkness flew to my hands, and anyone who looked at me would see nothing behind me but an endless black hole. No scythe on my side, either, but I didn't need one.

The Reaper stopped mid-motion, the shadows receding. Even he wouldn't attack another Reaper, even an unconventional one like me.

"Get out," he said. "Now."

I turned away and left the cottage in case he changed his mind about attacking me. So much for getting the local Reaper on my side. I closed the door behind me and marched downhill away from the cottage. My anger levels spiked, and I muttered some choice curses under my breath.

"Wow," said Mart. "That guy was scary. I hid outside in case he banished me."

"Depends what he can do without a scythe," I commented. "He was using it to hang his coat on, would you believe it? If I told the Reaper Council that, they'd confiscate it and probably put him on probation."

"*Are* you going to contact the Reaper Council?" he said.

"I don't know." On the one hand, the Reaper's incompetence had clearly caused a lot of hassle for the town's residents. On the other, I wasn't a snitch.

Besides, I'd rather do almost anything else than speak to the Reaper Council again.

"Well?" Mart flew alongside me. "Make your mind up. You'll have to decide soon if you're going to stay overnight or fly home with me."

"We can't all fly without a broomstick." My mind was stuck on the Reaper. If there's one thing I hated, it was loose ends. I didn't want to leave the town behind, and aside from the detective and the Reaper, everyone had been perfectly friendly so far... but the fact remained that this was not a good place to stay if one had a tendency to attract ghostly attention.

Then again, I'd already shown them—and the Reaper —what I was capable of. And I wasn't a quitter.

I retraced my steps to the restaurant, which had filled up with more people since I'd been gone. Carey waved me over from a table in the corner where she sat doing her homework with a small black cat perched on the chair opposite her.

"Hey." I pulled up a vacant seat, the smell of the food making me realise I was ravenous. "Who's he?"

"Casper is my familiar," she said. "He can see ghosts, but he's frightened of them, so he doesn't come ghost-hunting with me."

"Oh." I decided not to mention that a cat who was afraid of ghosts and a blogger who couldn't actually see them weren't a winning combination for a ghost-themed blog. She'd experienced enough disappointment today already. "My meeting with the Reaper didn't go well. He didn't care about Mrs Renner's ghost and wouldn't help. Threw a cigarette at me, too."

"Oh, that's horrible," she said. "My mum says he's a grumpy old man who deserves to be alone."

"Normally I give people the benefit of the doubt, but he's officially tied with Detective Drew as to who can annoy me the most today," I said. "And that's saying a lot."

"Didn't go well?" Allie joined us at the table. "Sorry. I didn't think Harold would listen to you, but it's always worth a try. I wondered if he might behave differently with someone who shares his gift for seeing ghosts."

"Does he throw things at all his visitors?" I asked.

"Oh, all the time," she said. "Sometimes he threatens to use his scythe on them, too."

"Even that's an improvement on using it to hang his coat on." I rolled my eyes. "He refused to answer a single question about Mrs Renner and claimed total ignorance of her death."

"He knows," she said. "Even if he wasn't the Reaper, he

lives next to the graveyard and he was there for her funeral."

"Doesn't mean he knows if her death was an accident or not, though," I said. "Who came to her funeral if she didn't have family?"

"A few polite residents from the local nursing home," said Allie. "None of whom she actually got along with when she was alive. Also, she does have family, but they aren't local and clearly aren't fond of her either. I'd feel sorry for the woman, but she was quite unpleasant to anyone who tried to be friendly to her and it doesn't surprise me that she's causing trouble from beyond the grave, too."

"Detective Drew doesn't seem to believe it," I commented. "How can he not believe in ghosts? He lives in a paranormal town."

I was getting more and more convinced that the detective was some busybody who had no business masquerading as a paranormal investigator, but I still hadn't the faintest clue what kind of paranormal he was.

"I spoke to him earlier and I'm not sure he doesn't believe in ghosts," she said. "But in Mrs Renner's case, no spirit has actually been seen."

So it was just me he had a problem with. Good to know. "Either way, there's going to be a problem if he keeps showing up at Mrs Renner's house and stopping anyone from getting rid of her ghost. Unless he has his own official ghost hunter on backup."

Allie blew out a breath. "He'll come around. He's not usually this suspicious of new visitors, and I don't want you to walk away feeling unwelcome here."

Hmm. I did have an idea of how to get inside the house

without being interrupted, but it meant tossing away my plan to spend as little time here as possible. "Everyone else I've met here has been lovely. I mean, except the Reaper."

"Glad to hear it." Allie gave me a bright smile. "Tell you what, you can order whatever you like off the dinner menu and I'll get Hayley to bring it to you. You've been stuck here all day because of this ghastly weather, after all."

I shouldn't stay any longer. I should fly home… but a warm bed and a hot meal sounded heavenly, and I never did have that drink.

I nodded. "All right."

————

A hot meal was just what I needed, and by late evening, I was starting to thoroughly enjoy myself. Hayley, whose shift had finished, came to join Carey and me at our table, followed by Allie herself. Casper lapped at a saucer of milk next to the table while the rest of us chatted about the latest result of the national Sky Hopper championships. I might remain estranged from the magical world, but that didn't make Mart and I any less prone to arguing about magical sports. It was nice to have someone living to talk to for once rather than rehashing the same old arguments with my stubborn brother.

"So are you staying in town?" Hayley asked.

"Just overnight," I said. "The rain threw off my schedule. I flew here on a broomstick, and I'm not up for getting blown off-course over Wales."

"There's a reason we don't have many flying contests

compared to some other magical communities," said Allie. "It's all this mist. Plays havoc with visibility."

Maybe if the ghosts went, so would the mist. Not that there was much chance of that happening with a nonentity of a town Reaper. It'd be a miracle if I could get rid of *one* ghost, especially with this so-called detective insisting on standing in my way.

"I bet." I finished my drink. "I think I'm going to have an early night."

Carey looked up. "Will you be staying in our inn, then?"

"I'm told there's a room with my name on it," I responded. "I should probably check in."

I wouldn't be going to bed for a while, but I needed to come up with a plan to get into that house other than wandering in that direction and hoping the detective wasn't there. The Reaper wasn't interested in the case, so there was zero chance of him being there, at least.

"You're leaving tomorrow?" Carey walked in step with me through the glass doors connecting the restaurant to the inn's reception area. "But… what about the ghost?"

"Detective Drew is more problematic," I said. "He'll probably be there first thing in the morning in all likelihood, so I doubt he'll let us get into the house. But I have an alternative."

"You're going after the ghost tonight," she said, the truth dawning on her.

"You bet." I cracked a grin. "Set your alarm. We have a ghost to catch."

5

While the bed in my hotel room was much more comfortable than the one back at my apartment, I didn't manage more than a power nap before my alarm woke me up for our midnight ghost-hunting mission. I rolled off the bed, smoothed my wrinkled clothes, and conjured up my warmest coat from back home with a wave of my wand. Then I went downstairs to meet Carey.

Mart flew alongside me. "You haven't asked if I had a nice nap, too."

I rolled my eyes. "I'm sure you found another guest to haunt."

He snickered. "It's a wasted opportunity. Why live in a town full of ghosts and not use it as a selling point?"

"Not everyone wants a ghost in their room, Mart." I climbed down the stairs into the hotel lobby. "Now shush. I don't want Carey to know you're here."

He pouted. "Why not?"

"Because you're a menace." And because she'd be put

out to say the least if I told her she couldn't share anything about him on her ghost blog. The risks of drawing the attention of the Reaper Council via that route were low, but they still existed.

He made a sceptical noise. "Have you asked her mother's permission to take her on a night-time ghost-hunting jaunt?"

"Of course I have." I was hoping that wouldn't turn out to be a bad idea. Given my previous experience with this particular ghost, it might be a risky move, but on the other hand, I didn't have the heart to leave Carey behind. I'd promised to let her record the experience for her blog, and besides, it would be a good idea to have someone to keep an eye out for trouble. Like that detective.

I halted, spotting Carey waiting in the lobby. The last thing we needed was for my brother's ghost to draw a trail of other unwanted spirits after us, but to my surprise, he held back and didn't get in my way for once. Maybe he'd taken my comments seriously… or he'd decided he'd prefer to haunt the hotel guests. Whichever.

"Hey, Maura." Carey wore her ghost goggles again, though she'd changed out of her school uniform into a thick coat and jeans. "Ready to go?"

"You bet." I led the way out of the automatic doors. "Let's go find us a ghost."

Carey was wide awake and skipped alongside me as I walked back towards the grand old house. Hardly anyone was on the streets—hardly anyone living, anyway—but Carey kept pulling her ghost goggles over her eyes and trying to identify any passing spirits.

"Was that a ghost?" She pointed at a nearby shadow.

"Nope, just a cat." I watched the black fluffy shape

saunter away. "Probably someone's familiar. Have you ever trained Casper to ghost-hunt with you? It might be worth thinking about."

She shrugged. "He's too scared. There are rooms at the inn he won't even go into."

"You could play up the whole ghost angle if you wanted to get more tourists to visit the inn," I told her. "I know that kind of thing is more popular with normals than it is with people like us, but it's worth a shot."

"Good idea." She halted in front of the manor house. "I'll ask my mum tomorrow."

The gate creaked open at my touch, and we walked through the garden to the front door. Carey hovered on the balls of her feet as she unlocked the door with her homemade key.

"Okay, we're in," I whispered. "I think we'll need to keep quiet if we want to get the ghost's attention without spooking her."

"Us, spooking her?" she said. "Shouldn't it be the other way around?"

"You'd be surprised." I doubted this ghost had any particular fear of the living, but a fair few spirits were terrified to face up to the fact that they were dead. It was the Reaper's job to convince them otherwise.

I was no Reaper, but I was the closest this town had to one, so the ghost would just have to deal with it.

"Mrs Renner?" I whispered into the dark hallway. I pulled out my wand and conjured up a spark of light in order to see where I was going. "Are you here?"

Silence. Carey edged into the hallway behind me, leaving the door partially open. I trod forward, using my wand to light my way, and caught sight of a human-shaped shadow in the middle of the hallway.

"Mrs Renner?"

I moved closer, but the shadow had vanished. With a flicker of unease, I recalled that this was the doorway where she'd met her untimely death. The frame had been cleared of debris, but parts of the ceiling looked unsteady to say the least. Maybe it'd been an accident after all and she had another reason for sticking around, but that didn't bring me any closer to convincing her ghost to move on to the world beyond.

A distinct thudding noise came from upstairs, like someone knocking into a heavy piece of furniture.

"Anyone up there?" I peered up into the gloom. The stairs were as dark as the rest of the house, as was the upper landing. No way was the detective stumbling around in the dark, so if the sound came from a person, it wasn't a living one.

The hairs rose on my arms, confirming my guess.

"Is she there?" Carey whispered.

"I'd say yes," I returned. "Stay close behind me."

She gripped both sides of her goggles and stuck to me like glue as I climbed the stairs. Silence followed us, though I kept my ears pricked for any further sounds from the ghost. My steps halted when I reached the top of the stairs, and a faint creaking noise came from nearby. I pressed my finger to my lips and took a step forward.

That's when my foot went through the floorboards.

"Ack." I stifled a yelp as the wooden boards scraped at my skin, and I found myself with one leg on solid ground and the other suspended in empty air.

Carey cried out. "Maura!"

"Hang on, I'm okay." I hopped forward on my other foot, but my knee had jammed in the hole in the floorboards, jagged wooden splinters pressing against my shin. "Stay back, or you might fall, too."

"But you're stuck." She caught my hands, and I half-shuffled across the floorboards, attempting to tug my leg out of the gap.

Something on the other side caught my foot and pulled back.

"Hey!" I kicked out at empty air, unbalanced, and my chin smacked into the floorboards, making stars flash before my eyes. The alarming thudding noises from below pushed me to the brink of using my Reaper powers to get out of the hole—but I wouldn't do that if I had any other choice in the matter.

Carey lost her grip on me, sitting down with a gasp. "There's someone coming upstairs."

I twisted around on the spot and saw a large hulking shadow at the foot of the stairs. This time, I didn't mistake it for a ghost, because it figured that the universe would send Detective Drew to torment me again. Just the person I wanted to see with my foot stuck in the floorboards and a cranky ghost on the loose.

"You again?" He tapped the light switch, banishing the darkness from the hallway and stairs.

"A little help, please?" I put on an ingratiating smile.

"What are you doing here?" He advanced upstairs, and Carey scrambled out of the way to let him pass by.

"Just hanging around." Almost literally. I shuffle-hopped forward in an attempt to tug my leg out of the hole and succeeded only in whacking my knee on the edge of the wooden board. The curse that escaped my lips made Carey blush furiously and the detective raise an eyebrow.

"I'd feel pity for you," he said, "but you're the one who trespassed in a deceased woman's home."

"It's not trespassing if you don't get rid of that ghost." I slumped down to catch my breath, and then looked up to find Detective Drew's outstretched hand ahead of me. "You're not going to give me a shove, are you?"

"Why would I do that?" He climbed past Carey, his hand still outstretched.

Oh, well. Not like I've got anything to lose at this point. I accepted his offered hand and let him help me tug my leg loose from the floorboards. I winced again when the boards scraped against my knee, and awkwardly placed my foot down on the top step. "Thanks."

"So you're not entirely without any manners."

"Shocking, I know." I held the banister for balance as I pulled myself upright. "Why are *you* here? Do you have nothing better to do with your time?"

"I had an inkling you might come back here, and it looks like my guess was right," he responded. "You're that sort."

I propped a hand on my hip. "Excuse me? What sort am I?"

Did I really want to know?

"Trouble." He stepped closer until we stood almost nose to nose.

Carey cleared her throat. "Um… what about the ghost? Was she upstairs?"

The detective broke his gaze away from mine and considered Carey. "Does your mum know you're out here in the middle of the night?"

"Yes," I told him. "I'm taking care of her."

He eyed the hole in the floorboards. "Right."

Annoyance flared within me. "Look, you don't believe in ghosts, but let me tell you that you have one seriously stubborn spirit in here. If you ever want this house to be habitable for anyone else, someone is going to have to get rid of it."

"And you're volunteering yourself for the cause out of the goodness of your heart?" His words dripped with sarcasm.

"What does it matter to you?" You'd think someone who worked as a paranormal detective would play nicer with other people. "You're the one who's investigating a murder without even considering speaking to the victim herself, despite the fact that I offered to help you do so. Out of the goodness of my heart." I returned his sarcasm in kind.

"You don't seem to be making much progress with her." He backed down the stairs, while I followed his path before our spirit took offence at him denying her existence by sending me flying downstairs or something.

Thankfully, the ghost stayed quiet. It seemed she was about as fond of the detective as I was—that is to say, not at all. He kept looking at me with that stern expression until I obligingly walked out of the front door into the garden, Carey trailing alongside me.

"How long have you been on this case, anyway?" I asked. "Because if all you're doing is hanging around her house and not questioning people who knew her, you won't get very far if you can't see her ghost."

His mouth tightened. "I came back to the house because her family has proven difficult to get hold of. It's taken a week for her grandson to get in touch and confirm he's coming to town to have a look at the house."

"So someone *is* going to inherit the house?" I asked. "Good to know. Might he have been the one who bumped off the old woman?"

"Don't be ridiculous," he said. "He's not from Hawkwood Hollow and didn't know she'd left no will dictating who gets her property until after her death. He didn't even come to the funeral, and he isn't due to arrive in town for another day."

"Doesn't make him innocent." In truth, I knew nothing about the guy, but anything that brought me one step closer to figuring out the reason for Mrs Renner's presence here was more than welcome.

"I'm not at liberty to discuss the details of my investigation with a stranger."

"Don't like outsiders, huh." I glanced at Carey. "Do you have *anyone* involved in your case who can actually see and talk to ghosts? Because I thought it was pretty standard."

Not strictly true. In most normal magical communities, the dead didn't stick around for long enough to be of any use in a murder investigation. But in a place like this, where the dead seemed to have taken up permanent residence here alongside the living, then you'd think the law enforcement would have adapted.

"Standard?" he echoed. "We don't get many homicides here at all. Not enough to make it worth involving outsiders and troublemakers."

My brow arched. "You mean the Reaper? What's his problem, anyway?"

He tutted. "I should have guessed you'd have decided to start bothering the other residents."

"She isn't bothering anyone," Carey protested.

"She's bothering me," said Detective Drew. "What possessed you to send her after that old fool of a gravedigger? Let me guess… he ordered you to leave, too."

"I see you've been taking tips from someone," I said. "He refused to talk to me, uses his scythe as an ornament, and when I tried to ask him if he had an apprentice to take over from him after his retirement, he threw a cigarette at me. He makes even you look like a gentleman. Why'd he stop doing his job?"

The detective pressed his mouth together. "Harold is a known recluse. You shouldn't have gone to visit him."

"Something is *wrong* in this town," I insisted. "There shouldn't be this volume of lost spirits wandering around."

"That isn't any of your concern," he said. "I should write you up for breaking into Mrs Renner's house— again—but I'm going to be generous and escort you back to the inn. And tomorrow morning, you're going to leave town."

"Says who?" I *had* planned to leave the following day, but his attitude got up my nose and made me want to dig my heels in. It wasn't wise, but he was either in denial and didn't want to know about the ghosts… or he had something to hide. Like everyone else here in Hawkwood Hollow, it seemed.

"Don't you have a job to go back to?" he said.

"Not that it's any of your business, but no, I don't." I didn't want to get into the *I got fired because a ghost disagreed with his family's funeral arrangements* discussion, not when he'd scoff and disbelieve me.

"She works as a ghost hunter," Carey put in. "Which is why I invited her here to begin with. Why are you being so mean to her?"

"Thank you!" I gave her a nod of genuine gratitude. "If you showed any signs of wanting to learn the truth about Mrs Renner's death, including speaking to her ghost, I'd leave you to it. But this town is spiritually constipated in a way I've never seen before."

"Spiritually *what?*" he said.

Okay. Maybe not the word I should have used if I wanted him to take me seriously. I wouldn't typically use such a term in front of a hot guy either, but his personality kind of made me forget that most of the time.

"I've been a ghost hunter most of my life," I said—technically true. "Normally, you don't get more than five ghosts in any given paranormal community at a time. In towns with resident Reapers, the number is closer to zero. And when it comes to the rare exceptions, people generally aren't resistant when I offer to help out. Maybe the witches and wizards who can see ghosts don't mind the constant disruption, but as for this house? It's haunted to its back teeth."

"You said you were here to get rid of *one* ghost," he said. "One who hasn't been seen."

"She chased off the construction crew." I looked to Carey for confirmation.

"They didn't leave the house because of a ghost," said the detective. "The renovators were forced to evacuate because half the ceiling collapsed when they tried to fix up the living room. They're coming back tomorrow with a specialist... *not* that that's an invitation to interfere."

I smiled. "Of course it isn't."

If there were renovators coming tomorrow, Detective Drew would have less freedom to march around giving everyone orders... and who knew, maybe they'd be grateful for my offer to assist them with getting rid of Mrs Renner's ghost.

He gave me a suspicious look. "What are you plotting?"

"Who says I'm plotting anything?" I walked towards the gate. "C'mon, Carey. Let's head back to the inn."

I waited for Carey to catch up, my knee still throbbing from where it'd scraped against the floorboards. Trust that detective not to be fooled by my leaving the scene earlier. Mart was nowhere to be seen, so I looked behind me to make sure he hadn't gone into the house and run afoul of the ghost.

The outline of a shadowy figure appeared in the upstairs window behind the detective. While one side of the window was boarded up, the other showed a dark bedroom... and a definite human-sized figure, transparent as glass. The hairs on my arms stood on end.

"Detective," I called out. "You might want to move away from the window."

He frowned at me. "What?"

The glass in the upper window shattered as a pile of wooden boards tumbled out, straight on top of Detective Drew.

I didn't stop to think. I whipped out my wand and cast a levitation charm on the wooden boards, running forwards in a futile attempt to reach the detective before the boards did. The gate slammed open and closed, and a gust of air set me stumbling right into the detective's arms. The boards clattered harmlessly to the ground, while Detective Drew looked down at me with his eyes slightly wider than before. It was the first time he'd looked at me with anything other than condescension in his expression.

I broke away from him, peering wildly into the hallway behind him. "Damn you, Mrs Renner. That was uncalled for."

"What are you talking about?" He eyed the wand in my hand. "Did you just knock those boards onto my head?"

"No, I levitated them *away* from you," I corrected. "That's one powerful ghost you've got in there."

He glanced at the pile of boards, then up at the window. "That's the third time one of those boards has broken. They're practically falling to pieces."

"You don't believe me." Again. Unbelievable. "Okay, I'll let them fall on your head next time."

And with that, I turned around and left through the gate once again. Carey hovered beside me, her eyes wide. "Did you see her? For definite?"

"I think I did," I said. "I definitely saw someone in that window, but I have no hope of getting her out as long as Detective Obstructionist is in my way. I don't think Mrs Renner is his biggest fan, either."

"I think we should go back," Carey said. "He might be in danger."

"Not if he's sensible and doesn't go back into the house," I said. "Besides, if the roof falls on him, he'll just come back as a ghost and insist it was an accident."

Her brow wrinkled. "If he's a ghost, he can't deny they exist, can he?"

"You might be underestimating his determination to prove me wrong."

Ungrateful, much? He could have at least thanked me for my attempt at stopping him from being knocked out cold. That's what I got for taking the initiative.

Carey gave a faint laugh. "You really get under his skin. That's what my mum said when she spoke to him earlier. I don't think he appreciated that comment."

"Maybe I should have asked her to tell him I left town." I sighed. "I guess there's no chance of me talking to the guy who inherited the house or anything?"

"Actually, you might be in with a shot," she said. "He's going to be staying at the inn. He arrives in town tomorrow morning."

I woke early, ready to talk to the person due to inherit Mrs Renner's house. In theory, anyway. Bright sunlight streamed in through the violet curtains, while the soft bed and comfy mattress made me reluctant to get up. Much nicer than my ratty old mattress back at my apartment. The inn itself was pretty nice in general, if you discounted the occasional ghost. Thankfully, the only one in my own room was the usual occupant.

"How did you sleep?" Mart asked. "I slept like the dead. Get it?"

"That wasn't funny the first seven hundred times you tried that one," I told him. "And I'd have slept better if I hadn't had a narrow brush with death at the hands of a ghost last night. You didn't happen to get a glimpse of her, did you?"

"Of course not," he said. "You and the detective stood outside nattering for so long that I came back here by myself."

"Couldn't you have looked around for the ghost?" I asked. "You might have been more likely to get through to her than me."

He put on a shocked face. "You'd have sent me after the ghost alone?"

"It's not like she could have done you any harm," I pointed out. "Which is more than I can say for the rest of us. If not for me, the detective would be in hospital with a concussion. Or worse."

"That's right, you saved his neck," said Mart. "Even though you hate him. Or so you say, anyway."

"I don't know why." I was too tired for this. "Instinct, I guess. Also, he did save me from falling through the floorboards."

He laughed. "Sure, and it's not at all because he's a hot detective who riles you up."

"Please don't say that," I said. "You're my brother. It's weird."

"I'm also dead, so I get free rein to comment on your love life for eternity. I don't make the rules." He floated away through the wall, humming the *Doctor Who* theme under his breath.

After a quick shower and a quicker conjuring spell to fetch a clean outfit from home, I went to the restaurant to grab breakfast and found a whole buffet laid out on rows of long tables. I spotted Allie standing near the end and made a beeline for her.

"How do I pay for this?" I asked.

"You don't have to pay for anything," she said. "You're here to help us."

"But... I haven't achieved anything yet." Not for lack of trying, but last night had hammered home how ill-prepared I really was. Especially for dealing with bad-tempered Reapers, detectives and ghosts all at once.

"You've done more than anyone else has," said Allie. "Mrs Renner's grandson arrives in an hour, by the way."

That gave me enough time to eat a decent breakfast, so I loaded a plate and sat down at a table. I was starving after last night's ghost-hunting misadventures, and it had been a long while since I'd woken up genuinely excited about getting to work. Even if this was a one-off and I wasn't an official ghost hunter, whatever I'd told Detective Drew.

I needed to do something about *him* if I had any intention of going back to Mrs Renner's house, but right now, I'd settle for explaining the situation to her grandson and hoping he was more likely to believe me.

I ate on my own, as Carey was getting ready for school and Allie was helping some new guests settle into their rooms. Hayley wasn't in, so the two of them must be handling everything alone. It seemed a lot to deal with, but from what I'd heard about the relative lack of tourists in town, the restaurant was their main business.

I mentioned this to Mart while I was milling around the lobby, waiting for Mr Renner to arrive.

"Most of the inn's rooms are empty," he responded. "If you ask me, they could double their business by offering a free ghost with every room. Everyone wins, including the ghosts."

"Have you found your calling, then?" I gave him an eye-roll. "I thought you didn't like it here."

"It's grown on me." He circled the lobby. "I like all this open space. It's not like that cramped apartment of yours."

"It's not cramped if you can walk through walls," I pointed out.

"Technically, so can you," he responded.

"Not without drawing the Reaper Council after me." I hadn't used my Reaper skills in years—aside from banishing ghosts, that is—but if the detective hadn't helped me out of that hole in the floor last night, I might have had to break that rule and mess with the laws of physics a little. The Reaper's number one rule: get the soul first, worry about everything else later, including the rules of nature. That's how Reapers can extract the souls of people killed in accidents at sea or crushed beneath falling buildings. On the other hand, let's just say ordinary people would be a little freaked out at the sight of me stepping through a wall of shadows and reappearing else-where. Even Carey. Better to save the party tricks for a last resort and stick with my wand.

The sound of footsteps on the stairs behind me cut through Mart's reply. Carey had entered the lobby, wearing her mustard-yellow school uniform. "Isn't Mr Renner here yet?"

"I think your mum said he'd be here soon."

Sure enough, we hadn't been there for a minute before the front door swung inward. A tall man entered the hotel, along with a woman who I assumed was his girl-friend or wife. He was a little older than I was, late twen-ties at most, and from the look of his sharp suit, he might have been whisked away in the middle of a business meet-ing. The woman wore similar attire. Her red hair was pulled into a tight ponytail and her nose held high as though she'd trodden in something foul.

"Hey, there!" Carey said brightly. "Are you Mr Henry Renner? And this must be Claudie, your wife."

"I am." Mr Renner looked down at her. "Who are you?"

"I'm Carey," she said. "My mum owns the inn."

"Then I assume you're here to carry my bags to my room." His gaze flickered to me. "Go on, run along."

Excuse me? "I don't work here." I kept my tone polite, with difficulty. "I'm here to talk to you about your grandmother's house."

"Oh, you're with the construction crew." If anything, his expression grew even more disdainful. "I've heard nothing but complaints about your shoddy work since it started, and now I've had to leave my office behind during our busiest season in order to ensure the house is fit for my wife and I to occupy. It's a disgrace."

"I'm not with the construction team either," I said, now thoroughly annoyed. "Did anyone tell you *why* the renovators keep being driven out of the house?"

"I assumed it was simple incompetence." He indicated his suitcase. "Aren't you going to carry that to my room?"

"Of course." Carey grabbed her wand and gave it a wave, and the suitcase vanished. "You're in room six. My mum will have your keys. She'll be here in a second."

Mr Renner and his wife walked to the desk. Allie popped up a moment later, engaging them in conversation.

"What a piece of work," I muttered to Carey. "He makes that detective look like a gentleman. Doesn't he know his grandmother's ghost is terrorising anyone who goes into the house?"

"I don't know," said Carey. "My mum said he was very rude to her on the phone, and it seems like he was pretty hard to get hold of, too. In the end, he only came here because he wants the house."

"That figures," I said. "I'd believe he bumped her off if he was the slightest bit enthusiastic about inheriting her house."

Then again, he struck me as the type of person who'd never been enthusiastic about anything in his life and had come out the womb loudly complaining about the state of the universe. I didn't particularly want to deal with him any more than I had to, but on the other hand, he was the most likely person to have a stake in the outcome of Mrs Renner's ghost being given the boot. As quickly as possible.

Detective Drew... I didn't know what *his* deal was, apart from his apparent need to get in my way at every step. But he wasn't a relation of Mrs Renner's, nor did he have anything to gain whether she stayed in the house or not. So I'd need to stay on this guy's good side—if he had one, that is.

Mr Renner pocketed the keys to his room and walked away from the desk, eyeing Carey and me. "You're still here? If you're not with the construction team, then who are you?"

A ghost hunter. An exorcist. Was there a professional word for someone like me? A non-official Reaper? "I'm here to help with the problems the construction company have been having with the property."

Namely, getting rid of the ghost of its former owner.

"Employed by whom?" He made for the door, followed by his wife.

"I work freelance." I turned back to Carey. "I don't

want to make you late for school. I'll tell you everything afterwards, okay?"

Her expression creased. "You're going to the house now?"

If I'm allowed in. Unfortunately, it didn't seem that Mr Renner would be much more help than the detective at letting me do my job. If he believed in ghosts, it would be an improvement, though he and his wife clearly wanted to be rid of me. "If I can. Should I walk you to school on the way?"

"I don't need to be at school for an hour," she added. "It's only up the road from the house, too."

"I'll drop you off after we look around the house, then," I said, and her expression brightened.

"You still haven't told me what your business is with the house," Mr Renner said to me.

"I was hired because I was told there's been a high level of spiritual disturbances on your grandmother's property." No sense in beating around the bush any longer. "As I witnessed for myself yesterday, the ghost of your deceased grandmother is still present, and is causing a great deal of trouble for the construction team trying to renovate the house."

"You're here because you think my grandmother's house is haunted?" He gave me a withering look. "What do you do, rattle a few boxes and then charge a bloody fortune for a bogus exorcism?"

"It isn't bogus, and I'm not charging you a penny," I said evenly. "I didn't even know you were coming to town until last night. A concerned citizen hired me to help out, as I have years of experience dealing with stubborn spirits."

"A likely story," he said. "Sounds more like excuse-making on the construction company's behalf, to make up for their gross incompetence."

"If you don't believe in ghosts, living in that house isn't likely to go very well for you," I told him. "Fair warning. A local detective tried to deny her existence and then the ghost threw a plank of wood onto his head."

"I think we should listen to her," said Claudie, his wife. "Maybe she's telling the truth."

"I doubt it," said Mr Renner. "I find it hard to believe a mere ghost could have caused enough delays in the construction work that I was forced to come here myself. Besides, I'm hearing that the issues with the renovation started long before she died."

"Huh." I hadn't known that. "I haven't met the people involved, so I wouldn't know about the specifics of the renovation issues. From what I've seen since I arrived here in Hawkwood Hollow, though, I don't blame the crew for leaving the house before one of them got hurt. Did you ever meet your grandmother while she was still alive?"

"Several times, but I didn't care for her," he said. "By all accounts, she was a miserable woman."

The apple doesn't fall far from the tree in that case, then. I managed to keep my mouth shut, with difficulty. "That may be, but if her ghost doesn't leave, it'll be too dangerous for you to live in her house. For that reason, I'm here to get rid of her."

Assuming she actually spoke to me this time, anyway. And assuming the detective didn't interrupt and start poking his nose where it didn't belong. Granted, it didn't sound like Mr Renner himself had hired a private investigator, so he couldn't be the person who'd asked Detective Drew to take over. He seemed entirely unbothered by the way his grandmother had died, accident or none.

"Let her come," said his wife. "It won't do any harm to have someone to help out in case the house really is haunted."

"Fine, but she'd better not get in our way." He quickened his pace, his shiny shoes slapping on the wet pavement.

Despite the town's bizarre numbering arrangement, he had no trouble finding the house, and opened the gate without hesitation. Then he reached under the porch and unearthed a key, before unlocking the front door.

"Oops," Carey whispered. "I didn't know there was a key hidden on the property."

"I guess he probably knows his grandmother's hiding places." Maybe he also knew how to lure out her ghost. You never knew.

Mr Renner pushed open the front door and entered the hallway, making a noise of disdain. "It's no wonder the place is falling to bits. Look at that. The wood's practically rotting away."

I peered at the door frame he indicated. I didn't see anything wrong with it, but then again, ghosts were my area of expertise, not construction issues. Though if the house really was falling to bits, had Mrs Renner known how bad it was? If she had, why had she stayed? Those were questions I needed to ask her ghost, assuming she showed her face, but who knew, maybe she'd stop terrorising people now her grandson had shown up. If she'd actually wanted him to have the house, which I still wasn't clear on.

Mr Renner prowled through the lower floor of the house, complaining about every inch of the place. I decided against mentioning that the construction crew weren't to blame for the majority of the issues—the house had only come under repair fairly recently, from what I'd figured.

"And just look at this." He slapped the door frame in the middle of the hall with the side of his hand. "What's it made of, cardboard?"

I peered through the frame to the other half of the hallway. While I'd scanned each room for any signs of the ghost, I hadn't explored it in-depth. Now I looked closer, it appeared the back section of the house had been added as an extension, as though someone with little knowledge of architecture had slapped the walls together without caring whether the foundations were sound or not. The door frame looked as though it'd been magically attached to the walls with a stickiness charm and nothing more, while the uneven ceiling exposed several roof beams. Maybe Mr Renner had a point.

He left the doorway and advanced down the hall, forcing Carey and I to back out of the way or else get knocked aside. "The construction crew ought to be here by now… and just what is that?"

"Ah." Carey and I exchanged glances, realising he'd spotted the hole in the floorboards at the top of the stairs where I'd fallen through the previous night.

Luckily for all of us, at that moment, there came a knock on the door.

"Finally," said Mr Renner, sweeping away from the stairs with his wife in tow. He wrenched open the door to reveal a mousy little man with whiskers that painted him as a rat shifter.

"Mr Renner?" Even his voice was rat-like and squeaky. "I'm Louis, the head of the construction work on your property. I am terribly sorry for your loss."

"So you're the one in charge of this disaster?" said Mr Renner, a contemptuous look on his face. "What do you have to say to me about the state of this house?"

"I am terribly sorry." His head bobbed contritely. "There was considerable trouble in the process, as your late grandmother was well aware of. We worked with her from the start on the renovations and continued after her death."

"And you did a lousy job, by all accounts," Mr Renner said. "Holes in the floor, collapsing supporting walls... and that's not even getting into the terrible neglect which caused the accident which led to her death. If I was a different man, I'd have you put away for this."

The rat shifter paled. "Sir, I can only tell you that it was a terrible, tragic accident... we warned Mrs Renner not to stay inside the house while the foundations were so fragile, and she claimed she intended to stay at the inn that day. She wasn't supposed to be at the property at all. That's why it took so long for us to realise she was there."

Huh. That's odd. I hadn't known Mrs Renner had been given a room at the inn while the construction was going on. Why would she have gone back to the house? That was a question to ask the ghost, if she ever showed up.

"Well, it's not good enough," Mr Renner proclaimed. "We came all this way only to find the house in such a state of disrepair that I have my doubts anyone has tried to fix the place at all. Are you going to help me or not?"

"Gladly, Sir, but allow me to explain the difficulty we've been having." Louis drew in a breath. "After your grandmother's death, we came to finish the job, but four of our best wizards quit the team, convinced that the ghost of your dead grandmother intended to have them killed."

"How absurd," he said. "If the house is really such a lost cause, then why were you so keen to invite me here?"

"Because… well." He hesitated. "Your grandmother wanted you to have it, and under the circumstances, nobody else wants to live here, not as long as the rumours continue."

I couldn't say I blamed them in the slightest.

"Then get in here and do your job, man," he snapped, backing into the hallway. "I expect an assessment. Tell me what is going on with this extension."

The two of them drifted into construction-related jargon, while I turned to Carey. "Was Mrs Renner definitely alone here when she died?"

"I honestly don't know," she whispered. "That's why my mum said we can't rule anything out. I *think* it was an accident, but as for why her ghost's sticking around—"

Mr Renner's raised voice carried down the hallway. "They think she was *murdered?* By neglect, for certain, but if anyone's to blame, it's the people who should have fixed up this house. Just look at the state of that wall."

I made a mental note to ask him if he was aware there was a self-proclaimed paranormal detective already on the case, but now was definitely not the time to bring up that subject. If Mr Renner didn't think his grandmother had been murdered, though, then who had hired him? I had to admit, it was gratifying to think that for all Detective Drew's claims that he was more welcome at the house than I was, that clearly wasn't the case in Mr Renner's eyes. He didn't think her death was anything more than an accident caused by the dilapidated state of the old house.

I was debating sneaking upstairs for another look around for our missing ghost, when Carey grabbed my arm. "Look!"

I spun to face the doorway to one of the ground-floor rooms, where a plank of wood was hovering in mid-air as though levitated by a spell.

"Um," I said. "Mrs Renner?"

The wooden plank continued to hover in the air. Then a yelp came from one of the rooms further down the hall-way. Uh-oh.

"Carey, stay behind me," I said. "Mrs Renner, can you tell me what the issue is? Do you want them to leave?"

The wooden plank dropped to the floor, and Mr Renner's swearing from the next room intensified. I left the room at a run, Carey on my heels, and skidded to a halt.

A grey-haired woman blocked my path—wild-eyed, transparent, and furious.

7

Carey yelped and hid behind me as a tremendous gust of wind blew open every door in the house. Mrs Renner's ghost flew up through the ceiling and out of sight, while I ran down the hallway to find the rat shifter looking around the living room in bafflement. Behind him, Mr Renner hopped around rubbing his foot. "That is the last straw. Who moved that sofa?"

The sofa in question lay several feet away from where it had once been, and I had an inkling I knew who the culprit was.

"Mr Renner," I said, "your grandmother's ghost was just here a second ago. I think she wants to talk to you."

He put down his foot, his eyes narrowing. "Are you mocking me?"

"Of course I'm not," I said. "She just blew all the doors open and then flew upstairs."

"I saw the wooden beam floating," added Carey, her voice slightly awed. "That was her, wasn't it?"

"You *saw* the ghost?" said Louis. "Excuse me, young lady, but who are you?"

"We're here to get rid of the ghost," said Carey, with more initiative than I'd have expected considering the scare she'd just had. "Maura's an expert ghost-hunter. And I'm her assistant."

Mr Renner made a rude noise. "Nonsense."

The rat shifter looked as awed as Carey did when he studied me. "You've seen her? Whereabouts?"

At least one person believed me. I pointed into the hallway. "There, but she flew up through the ceiling."

"Aren't you going to go after her, then?" Mr Renner said, his tone tinged with sarcasm, which I ignored.

I pulled out my wand. "I'll see how unstable it is up there first."

While I could use my wand or even my broomstick to fly upstairs, that didn't mean the ghost wouldn't be able to knock me out of the air and force me to use my Reaper powers. But I'd have to take the risk if I wanted answers from her. Whether her death had been an accident or not remained to be seen, but I'd seen her up close for the first time, and I wanted to know why she'd decided to show her face now.

Carey tagged along behind me to the stairs. "Are you sure?"

"I am, but can you keep an eye on things down here?" I held up my wand, eyeing the stairs. "I'd rather neither of us fell through the floor this time, and I can't watch both of us *and* the ghost at once."

She blinked. "But..."

"Please." I dropped my voice. "It's lucky you weren't the one who got stuck in the floorboards last time. She's dangerous, and I reckon she'd be more likely to talk to me alone."

She held up the ghost goggles. "Can you take these with you?"

"I'd better not," I said. "These aren't good conditions for filming, and it might make her even less inclined to open up to me. Besides, I won't banish her yet."

She bit her lip, then nodded, probably figuring that filming the ghost during the day with Mr Renner storming around in the background wouldn't have anywhere near the impact of doing the filming at night-time. Not that Mr Renner was likely to be pleased with the idea of Carey using his home to make videos for her ghost blog and putting them on the internet either way.

I'd leave *that* for later. For now, I climbed the stairs, moving quickly over the threadbare carpet and avoiding the nails sticking out of the wooden planks. I kept my wand out ready to cast a quick levitation spell in case the floor collapsed again. Reaching the landing, I hopped over the ruined section of floor, and peered into the grand bedroom through the nearest door. "Mrs Renner?"

No reply. I scanned the room and then moved onto the next. Most seemed to be guest rooms, and the upstairs looked a lot sturdier than the lower floor. Smaller, too, and less patchy. I recalled the construction workers saying something about an extension being added afterwards...

The hairs on the back of my neck rose as a chill blew through the landing. Then a petulant voice whispered, "Why can't you leave me alone?"

I tensed, shadows stirring around me before I could reel them in. "I'm not here to harm you."

"Then get out of my house." The old woman appeared

before me, her transparent form flickering around the edges.

I stood my ground, reluctant to bring out my Reaper powers until I was sure there was no other option. After all, once I sent her to the afterlife, she wouldn't be coming back, and I could say goodbye to any shot I might have had at finding out if her death had been an accident or not. That detective would lose his chance at answers without even seeing her. Not that I was doing this for him. The whole situation weirded me out, and I knew there was something odd about both her death and her ghost's appearance here.

The breeze intensified as she moved closer and the floorboards creaked beneath my feet. Was she doing that? It was hard to tell, but from what she'd done to the window yesterday, she was way more powerful than the average spirit.

Shadows flowed around my feet and up to my hands. The ghostly figure of the old woman narrowed her eyes at me. "Your shadows don't scare me. You won't Reap *my* soul."

So she did know what I was. No surprise, since I hadn't been nearly careful enough to hide it. "I won't have to Reap your soul if you'd just tell me why you're here."

"I stayed because I belong here, and this is my house," she said. "The Reaper has a new apprentice, does he?"

Shadows surrounded me like a cloak as a chill breeze nipped at my skin. "No, I'm here on my own. I want to know if your death was an accident or not."

"They all say it was an accident," she snarled. "They say I was a foolish old woman who shouldn't have been in the house at all. They say I should have left twenty years ago. The house is mine."

"Why were you here, then?" I asked. "What were you doing downstairs when you died? Was anyone else around?"

"Dolores," she snapped. "Dolores Malone was here."

"Who is Dolores Malone?"

"My mortal enemy."

Right. Of course she had an enemy. A whole list of them, in all likelihood. People like her were more likely to stick around after death for the sake of revenge than for any other reason.

"So you came back to the house to see this Dolores Malone person?" I pressed. "Why?"

"Because I wouldn't have put it past her to burn this place to the ground while I wasn't here," she said. "She was always showing up on my doorstep and hassling me, telling me I should be in the retirement home and not in this old house."

"You came back to the house when it was in the middle of dangerous construction work because you were afraid your alleged mortal enemy would knock it down when you weren't there?" I couldn't keep the scepticism out of my voice.

Mrs Renner's ghost straightened upright. "I don't have to explain myself to the likes of you, Reaper. If you think you can play mind games with me—"

"I'm not here to play mind games, I'm here to discern the circumstances of your death," I said. "So I can get that paranormal detective off the case. Who hired *him*, anyway?"

"What's going on?" Mr Renner shouted upstairs.

The ghost vanished from sight. The floorboards gave another creak, causing me to jump backwards.

"I found your grandmother, but you just scared her off." I backed to the stairs, careful to avoid the gap in the floorboards. "She said her death wasn't an accident."

She'd also named a potential culprit, but I'd reserve judgment until I knew more about this Dolores Malone person. Wand in hand, I reached the top of the stairs. Mr Renner and his wife stood at the bottom, with Carey hovering behind them.

Mr Renner glared at me as I descended the stairs. "Well? What have you learned?"

"Apparently, someone called Dolores Malone was your grandmother's mortal enemy when she was still alive," I said. "Your grandmother claimed she was the reason why she was at the house the day she died. She thought this Dolores person was going to demolish the place. Any idea who she is?"

"No idea," he said in sour tones.

"I do," said Louis the rat shifter. "Dolores Malone is a witch who lives in the town's retirement home. I heard she and Mrs Renner didn't get along, but she was far from the only person who had a quarrel with her."

Hmm. Given Mrs Renner's accusation, it was worth looking into. It was the first lead I had from the mouth of the old woman herself, which had to be worth something. Right?

"And did my grandmother's ghost have anything else to say about the state of the place?" Mr Renner gave the rat shifter a withering look.

"No," I said. "She didn't mention the construction workers at all."

Carey tugged at my sleeve. "I'm late for school, too. I'd better run."

"I'll walk you there," I said, all too happy to get away from Mr Renner. "I'll be back later if I learn anything new."

Mr Renner grunted in a disinterested manner. I'd made a mental note to talk to the rat shifter later, too, but the poor guy had enough going on and I doubted he'd intended to kill the old woman. Not if he'd known he'd end up dealing with her equally unpleasant grandson afterwards.

I left them to it, walking with Carey to the gate and out into the street.

"Sorry," she said. "I'd skip school again, but my mum won't let me get away with pretending to have flu twice in a week."

"Don't worry about it." I let her lead the way down the street, and we left the old manor house behind. "You didn't mention Mrs Renner was supposed to be staying at your family's inn when she died."

She looked down. "My mum tried to convince her to stay, but she wasn't having any of it. We didn't want word to spread in case people started talking. The inn is our family's only source of income, and we get so few visitors as it is."

"I won't tell anyone," I said, "but Mr Renner doesn't seem like the reasonable type. He was already threatening poor Louis."

"I know." She bit her lip. "Mrs Renner wanted to stay

in the house all the time and didn't want anyone else to butt in. She didn't even like the construction workers being there."

Hmm. "How well did you know her while she was alive?"

"Not that well," she said, "but people at the restaurant always gossip, and everyone said her constant complaining kept driving away everyone who tried to work on the house."

"Now it's her ghost driving people away instead," I remarked. "And at this rate, Mr Renner will end up doing the same. If he decides to stay here, anyway."

He hadn't said if he'd been the one who'd hired Detective Drew as a paranormal investigator, either. If not, the two of them might well end up in a standoff which would provide some entertainment if nothing else, but it wouldn't bring me any closer to figuring out why her ghost was being so damn stubborn.

I escorted Carey up to the gates to the local witch academy, a cheerful building painted magenta with bronze features.

"I'll see you later," she said. "Are you going back to Mrs Renner's house now?"

"I think I'll have a word with this Dolores Malone first," I said. "To see if she agrees with the *mortal enemies* comment, and if she really did go to Mrs Renner's house the day she died."

"I can't believe you talked to her." She removed the ghost goggles from her head and slipped them into her school bag, her mouth pinching. "I wish I'd been able to see."

"Maybe next time." Without the natural ability to see

ghosts, it was unlikely… and really, I was supposed to be getting rid of old Mrs Renner, not making conversation with her.

But I kept forgetting that to Carey, seeing the ghost *was* the point, and I'd unintentionally cut her out of it in a bid to keep her out of danger. She was old enough to make the choice for herself, however young she seemed, and I kept forgetting that, too. Maybe it was because when I'd been her age, nobody had given *me* the choice. It was ghost hunting or nothing when you were in a Reaping family.

I did my best to shove the bad memories aside as I began my search for the town's retirement home.

"Boo." Mart flew behind me. "You're finally out of that awful house?"

"For now," I said. "Let me guess… you went walkabout when I was upstairs talking to Mrs Renner's ghost?"

"She actually spoke to you this time?" he said. "What did you do, threaten to Reap her soul?"

"Nope, I just asked if her death was an accident," I said. "She said it wasn't. She also threw the blame at her so-called mortal enemy, who I'm on my way to see right now."

I filled him in as we walked. Mart couldn't go too far from me, but he'd certainly made himself busy exploring the town whenever he hadn't been at my side. As a result, he was able to lead me straight to the retirement home, which was painted in similar magenta shades to the academy. And… haunted. Really haunted. No fewer than seven ghosts flocked over to me when I walked up to the burgundy-painted door and knocked.

A female goblin wearing a green cloak answered the door. "Can I help you?"

"I'm looking for Dolores Malone," I said. "I'm Maura, and I'm from out of town."

"Dolores?" she called. "Someone's here to see you."

An old woman with curly white-blond hair hobbled up to the door, looking at me through watery eyes. "I don't know you. Not one of my grandchildren, are you?"

"I doubt it," I said. "Is there somewhere we can talk?"

"Talk?" she said. "Outside. There's a place in the back garden where I like to sit."

I glanced at the goblin nurse, but she was already distracted by a pair of old wizards tussling over a remote control. Dolores led me through a living room full of people sitting in armchairs watching TV, playing board games, and reading books. It would have been a nice cosy setting, if not for the number of ghosts staring at the TV or mournfully trying to turn the pages of the books. A fair few of the residents acknowledged their presence, whether through looking in their direction or via talking to them directly. Being able to see ghosts tended to be more common among older witches and wizards, in my experience.

Dolores walked out of the open door into the back garden and sat down at one of the white plastic tables outside. "What did you want to speak to me about?"

"I'm here to talk to you about Mrs Renner," I said. "I'm told she thought you might pay a visit to her house at the time she died."

"Visiting me?" She cupped her ear. "No, she never visited me. Never left that awful house of hers."

"Um, I meant to ask if you were visiting *her*," I said a

little louder. "At her house. Were you there on the day she died?"

"No, of course not," she said. "The only time I left the retirement home that day was to go to my appointment with the hairdresser. I remember because it was raining."

"Are you sure?" I asked.

She sounded confident enough, but her comment about me being one of her grandchildren had made me wonder if her memory wasn't the most reliable.

"Of course I'm sure." She jerked her head at the goblin nurse, who was talking to another old woman behind us. "Ask Frankie. She took me to the appointment."

"Hmm." I cast my mind around for other questions to ask. "Mrs Renner said you two weren't friendly with one another. What was your history together?"

"History?" she echoed. "She always had to have the last word. Vindictive, she was. Stubborn. We were in the same coven, you know, and she never did play well with others. But I wasn't there when she died, and I had nothing to do with her tragic accident."

The goblin nurse stopped by our table. "Everything all right?"

"Yeah, I'm just leaving now." I rose to my feet. "Thanks for letting me come here."

Frankie walked with me to the door, as though she thought I might sneak back in. "You're not a relation of hers?"

"No, I... I'm working on behalf of Mrs Renner and her grandson. I just needed to ask a couple of questions about her death."

The goblin's expression turned frosty. "Are you with the police? You should have said."

"Not with the police." I really should have come up with a better cover story. Or just left the detective work to Drew. "I'm trying to find out who was around when Mrs Renner died. She mentioned Dolores's name—"

"Dolores wasn't there," the goblin insisted. "I said the same to the man who came here earlier."

"A man came here?" I said. "Detective type, by any chance?"

"Friend of yours, is he?" Her expression melted a little, and a flush spread across her cheeks.

"Nope," I said. "Definitely not. I had a run-in with him this week already. I'm not a detective, but I've been hired to banish Mrs Renner's ghost. She's sticking around the house and refusing to leave, so I wondered if there was a reason for it. Often, ghosts stay put because of unfinished business."

"Dolores didn't kill her," the goblin insisted. "Nobody did. Her death was an accident, though it wouldn't surprise me if she was crafty enough to stick around telling everyone she was murdered."

"Ah." Might she be telling the truth? I hadn't had a long enough conversation with Mrs Renner to gauge whether she'd go as far as to tell a lie of that size, but given what I'd seen of her personality, it wasn't an impossible notion that Dolores was innocent and Mrs Renner was trying to stir up trouble from beyond the grave. Unless Frankie was covering for her, that is, but that seemed unlikely, too.

"Thanks anyway," I added. "I hope I can lay her spirit to rest."

"I hope so, too." The goblin cast a glance behind her. "None of us rest easy in this place, it seems."

I probably wouldn't get any more answers from

Dolores Malone, so I turned to head back the way I'd come. I wondered about returning to Mrs Renner's house, but as soon as the thought crossed my mind, I spotted someone on the other side of the road, heading in the same direction.

Detective Drew. Just who I needed to see today.

8

I'd hoped the detective wouldn't spot me, but it seemed that was too much to ask of the universe. He crossed the road the instant he caught sight of me and halted in front of me.

"You again," he said. "I think we got off on the wrong foot earlier."

I made a sceptical noise. "You think?"

"Consider what it looked like," he said. "You broke into a dead woman's house… twice."

"So did you," I said. "Her family didn't hire you. So who did?"

His mouth pressed together. "Who told you her family didn't hire me?"

"The woman herself did," I said. "So did Dolores Malone."

"So that's why you went to the retirement home," he said, looking slightly disgruntled. "I'm not obligated to disclose my client's personal information."

"If she's dead, it shouldn't matter," I pointed out. "What

possible stake might you have in this? Why do you care if her house is sold or not?"

"Why are *you* so interested in this case?" he asked.

Oh, come on. I had a headache, I'd had a rotten day, and I was no closer than before to figuring out whether Mrs Renner's death had been an accident or not. Fine, then. I'd give him the truth. "I'm broke. Carey's mum promised to pay me for banishing her ghost. That's it."

"You're really a ghost hunter?" he said. "That's what you do for a living?"

"Yes, why?" I folded my arms across my chest. "I already told you. You could use someone like me here in Hawkwood Hollow, since your Reaper is neglecting his duty. If he'd escorted Mrs Renner's ghost into the afterlife after her death, I wouldn't have needed to come here."

"But you have yet to banish her," he observed. "Instead, you're wandering around talking to the town's citizens."

"I thought you didn't believe she was a ghost." I met the challenge in his eyes, and a spark of energy zinged between the two of us. "Make up your mind."

"Investigating her death is *my* job." He didn't break his stare from mine, and I suppressed the urge to look away. "In any case, Dolores seems to have an ironclad alibi, as I found when I questioned her earlier."

"Despite her enmity with Mrs Renner," I added. "Who else did she have on her list?"

He cocked a brow. "List?"

"Of enemies," I said. "People like her always have a list. She called Dolores her mortal enemy, so I figured there must be others."

"You went to her house earlier?" he said. "Did you ingratiate yourself with her grandson, by any chance?"

Of course he'd know Mr Renner was in town. "I wouldn't say that. He's as bad as his grandmother was, if not worse. I don't blame her for dropping a sofa on his foot."

"I thought your purpose was to banish her ghost," he said. "If she's as active as you claim, why is she still in the house?"

"She vanished before I could get rid of her, but I thought it was worth speaking to Dolores first," I said. "To see how much truth there was to Mrs Renner's claims that she was involved in her death. Mrs Renner seemed to think Dolores was at the house when she died, but Dolores herself claimed otherwise."

His brows drew together. "I spoke to Dolores myself because the two were known to have a contentious relationship, but I didn't know Mrs Renner thought Dolores was present at her death. What did she say?"

"Dolores claimed she was at the hairdressers instead," I said. "Frankie—the nurse who took her to her appointment—backed her up. I guess Mrs Renner might have been lying about her being there, but that takes me back to square one."

"Then perhaps you should speak to her again," he said.

"What, Mrs Renner?" Wait a moment. "Are you volunteering to come ghost-hunting with me?"

His gaze drifted in the direction of the house. "Perhaps she'll be more likely to show her face with an authority figure around."

I gave a mock gasp. "Detective, do you actually believe me?"

"I don't see what you'd have to gain from lying, if you're as broke as you claim you are," he said.

"There's no need to rub it in," I said. "The situation in this town goes way beyond Mrs Renner, but she's all I'm here for. And right now, I'm sure her death *was* an accident, despite her enmity with Dolores. So I need to convince her ghost of that and send her on her merry way."

His mouth pressed together. "There's something not quite right about that house. Ghost or no ghost."

"Mr Renner said the same," I said. "He's still at the house right now. Did *he* hire you?"

I already knew he probably hadn't, or else he'd have mentioned the detective earlier when he'd been complaining about the house's seemingly endless list of flaws.

"No." At least he'd answered me this time, but he didn't elaborate on his answer. Though with him on my side, it'd be much easier to find out whether Mrs Renner was a murder victim or just a troublesome ghost out to deceive people.

We walked back to the house together. I heard Mr Renner's raised voice even before we reached the property, which sounded like he was giving that poor rat shifter another tongue-lashing. I halted outside the gate. "I think someone screwed up again."

"How could you mess up something so simple?" Mr Renner's voice rang through the open window.

I arched a brow at Drew. "Still want to go in there?"

"Let's see what he's angry about first." He went through the gate, and I let him take the lead, more than happy to let someone else deal with Mr Renner. Upon opening the door, Drew halted in front of the living room door. The rat shifter, Louis, cowered next to the ruins of a collapsed cabinet, and at his side stood two equally fright-ened-looking wizards, holding wands in their hands.

"What seems to be the matter here?" said Drew in his most authoritative voice.

Mr Renner wheeled on him. "This incompetent excuse for a construction worker and his even more incompetent staff just wrecked this priceless piece of antique furniture. I specifically asked them to levitate it out the window to avoid any accidents. Instead, they dropped it on the floor."

Uh-oh. If I had to hazard a guess, it seemed Mrs Renner was at it again. "Sorry to hear that. It looks like your grandmother's ghost is back."

He swore. "You mean to say she's still here? I thought you got rid of her."

"I thought she left," I said. "I was under the impression she disappeared after we spoke earlier, but maybe she objected to you removing her furniture."

He grunted. "If she doesn't want me to sell her furni-ture, she'll have to try harder. You, rat shifter, take your people back in there and bring out the rest of the furni-ture, and try not to break anything this time."

"Maybe you should avoid removing anything from the house until she's gone?" I suggested.

"I'm not staying here any longer than I have to," he retaliated.

At least it seemed clear he had no intention of actually living inside the house. Which was good news for the other residents of the town. Not so much for Mrs Renner, however.

One of the wizards backed away from the fallen cabi-net. "I can't tell you how sorry I am—"

"Quiet," he snapped. "This is an absolute disgrace. I should order you to pay for the damages."

Detective Drew stepped in to speak to Mr Renner. "With your permission, Maura and I would like another opportunity to speak to your grandmother."

I barely stifled my surprise. He'd decided to act as though we were working together? Or maybe he'd constructed a cover story to tell Mr Renner so that we'd both have an excuse to be here, while I used my ghost-whispering skills to get answers from Mrs Renner about the manner of her death. Either way, I wasn't complaining about having someone else on my team.

"Are you going to get rid of her this time?" Mr Renner enquired.

"Provided we can gain concrete answers as to whether her death was accidental or not," Drew interjected. "From what Maura here told me, she stayed behind in the house for a reason."

"She's strong," I added, hardly able to believe he'd actually taken my side. "Strong enough to levitate and break heavy objects, by the look of things. That means she's likely to put up a fight when I try to banish her. If I try to calm her down first, I'm more likely to be able to get conclusive answers and cause less damage to the house."

"I thought you went to talk to a witness," Mr Renner said. "What did this person have to say?"

"The witness wasn't actually at the house when she died," I said. "Your grandmother told me she was the reason for her presence at the house at the time of her death, but she might have been mistaken."

Or lying. What she'd have to gain from that, I had no

idea. Maybe she just wanted to take poor Dolores down with her.

He grunted. "Given the state of this place, she shouldn't even have been in the house to begin with. It's been uninhabitable for at least a few months, if not more. If this person convinced her to come into the house anyway, then I will have words to say to them."

"She didn't," I said. "She had an alibi."

"Regardless, we need proof your grandmother's death was an accident before I can drop my investigation," said Drew. "With your permission, Maura and I will go and see if there are any signs of Mrs Renner's presence around the house."

Who are you and what did you do with Detective Drew? I hadn't the faintest idea what to add to that, so I pulled out my wand and walked with him to the stairs.

"Is that all you have?" he asked. "No ghost-hunting gear like your blogger friend?"

"Carey?" I pictured her goggles. "No, I'm not sure that stuff really works. And I do have gear."

Namely, my Reaper powers. Which I didn't generally show off in front of a living audience. Especially someone who was being cagey to say the least as to who had hired him, and was still, technically, a suspect. Even if he'd finally come around to my viewpoint, sort of.

The detective didn't look convinced. "If you're sure you can handle her, then we'll go upstairs."

"Watch out for holes in the floorboards," I warned. "I can levitate one of us at a time, but probably not both at once."

"So you're a witch as well as a ghost hunter," he said. "Not a local coven?"

"Nope." I *really* didn't want to talk about my ex-coven. "I've never been to Hawkwood Hollow before."

"Right, you said," he said. "So you're certain she'll speak to you?"

"If she doesn't object to you coming with me," I said. "If you need me to ask her any particular questions, then give them to me and I'll see if I can get answers."

"Did she explicitly say she was murdered when you spoke to her earlier, then?" he asked.

"She said her death wasn't an accident," I said. "She also said Dolores was the reason she was here at the house when she died, which we now know to be a lie. Unless Dolores cancelled on her or something."

But that didn't fit with their general enmity with one another. Why would someone who hated her pay a social call? No... there was definitely something missing in what I'd heard from Mrs Renner so far. I was more inclined to take Dolores's word as truth, but if I wanted to get the ghost on my side, I'd have to refrain from doing anything that might tick her off.

As if on cue, a rattling wind came through the hallway, making me shiver. *Is she listening to us right now?*

"Without direct confirmation from her, we can't be sure," he said. "Also, taking the testimony of a ghost on behalf of an outsider isn't my usual method of gathering evidence."

"I gathered." He might never have seen a ghost before, but he definitely knew *something* about the weirdness going on in town. That, however, would be a question for later. "Though I'm surprised, given how many other ghosts are here. I guess it's rare that someone's death isn't an accident, so there'd be no need to consult any ghosts."

He cut me a sideways glance. The breeze started up again, whistling overhead. "Murder is a rarity here, yes. Hawkwood Hollow is a small, close-knit community, for the most part."

"Are you new in town, then?" I asked.

He tilted his head. "Is now the best time for this conversation?"

"Just wondering if you're going to continue to get in my way."

His brows rose. "I could say the same for you."

"Hey, I'm not in your way now," I said. "I'm offering to help you."

That is, if our ghost ever showed up. I placed a foot on the bottom stair, which gave a creak.

"I'll catch you if you fall," he said.

That was… more reassuring than I'd have expected. "I'll hold you to that."

I climbed the stairs quickly, hopping over the hole in the floorboards and heading for the part of the landing where I'd spoken to the ghost earlier. Drew followed closely behind me, which made me jittery for reasons I couldn't put my finger on. Maybe because now he seemed to believe me, and I wanted to give him conclusive proof of my ghost-hunting talents.

As for the Reaper abilities, though… I'd rather not show *them* off in front of him. A cold breeze whistled through the roof beams. Then one of the bedroom doors slammed.

"Uh-oh," I said. "I think she's realised she has company."

"*Leave, now,*" her voice echoed throughout the house.

The wind struck up again, louder this time, and there came a crash from downstairs, followed by a scream.

My heart gave a lurch, and I looked at Drew. "Did you hear that?"

He nodded. "I did. Someone screamed downstairs. A woman."

Who? The construction workers were all male, but I hadn't seen Mr Renner's wife earlier. She must be somewhere inside the house.

I ran to the stairs and took them two at a time down into the hallway. As Drew caught me up, I opened the door to the living room. There, I found Mr Renner's wife lying beneath the sofa, which hovered a foot off the ground.

"Mrs Renner!" I shouted. "Stop that at once."

I flicked my wand and the sofa flew into the air, smacking into the wall with a thud and dropping to the floorboards. Claudie climbed to her feet, shaking all over.

"Thanks," she gasped. "I was sitting on the sofa when it fell out from underneath me, as though someone yanked it across the floor."

I gave the sofa a stern look. "Really, Mrs Renner?"

"The others are outside," said Drew.

Claudie followed Drew out of the house, and I ran behind her in case Mrs Renner started throwing things again. In the front garden, the construction workers gathered below the window which had broken the previous night.

"What is going on?" Mr Renner bellowed.

"The ghost," I said in explanation. "Why did you leave your wife alone in there?"

As Claudie headed over to talk to him, I turned to one

of the renovator wizards. "I'm starting to see why you had so much trouble making progress on the renovation work."

"Oh, it's not just since she died," he said. "The house's very foundations are flawed. It's only getting worse, too. If I didn't know better, I'd say there's a spell at work, especially on that extension."

"A spell… on the house?" I frowned. "Don't get me wrong, this place is clearly falling to bits, but everything I've seen so far has been caused by a ghost."

Except her death… which had been caused by the door frame collapsing on top of Mrs Renner herself.

"We've tried to call in a specialist to see if the place was under a hostile spell," he added. "But she died before he showed up, and now the place is haunted, he won't set foot in there."

"You think someone put a spell on the house?" I asked. "Something that caused her death? Who would have done that?"

Dolores had said she hadn't been there when Mrs Renner had died… but she'd visited before. Mrs Renner had said so. And she could have used the spell at any time, in theory.

"The signs are there, but we haven't found where it started," he explained. "If it was a simple hex, then any sign pointing back to whoever cast it would have disappeared by now. Even if it was a curse, the person who cast it would have only needed to hit part of the house for the rest of it to be affected. Otherwise, no traces would be left behind."

Well, that's inconvenient. It fit with what I knew about curses and hexes, but I'd never heard of one being used on a house before. He was probably right, though… the odds of any evidence being left behind to point back to the person who'd actually cast the spell were low.

"I had the impression that the renovations started weeks or months before she died," I said, addressing the group as a whole. "Were there problems from the start, or did it happen at a specific point in the project?"

Before anyone could reply, a tremendous crash sounded. As I turned in the direction of the house, a loud scream came from inside. A teenage girl's scream.

I ran to the front door and opened it, Drew behind me. "That sounded like…"

"Carey?" I called out. "She's supposed to be at school. I already dropped her off at the academy."

Had she come back here after all? I moved through the hallway, following the direction of the noise, until I came to the kitchen at the back of the house. The back door, which I hadn't acknowledged before, lay open, and a figure lay outside, surrounded by a scattering of roof tiles.

It was old Dolores Malone, and she was dead.

9

Drew retreated down the hall to speak to the others. I, meanwhile, scanned the kitchen for the source of the scream until I spotted a small figure concealed beneath the table.

"Carey?"

She crawled out from under the table and straightened upright, her eyes wide and frightened. "She's dead!"

"I know. Let's get you out of here." I beckoned to her and she hurried to my side, not looking back at the body in the garden. "Did you see what happened?"

"No, but I heard a crash, and when I looked outside to see what was going on..." She blinked hard. "I thought they'd blame me if they found me beside her body."

"We don't, but we'd like to know what happened." I stepped aside to let Mr Renner, his wife, Drew and the others enter the kitchen, and we all made our way through to the garden.

Outside, Dolores Malone lay sprawled in a pile of fallen roof tiles. Above, the roof was half-bare, as though they'd slid off of their own accord. A chill raced down my back. *Did Mrs Renner do that?* Had she thought she was getting revenge on her so-called nemesis for her own untimely death?

A head popped up behind the chimney, and the rat shifter stared wide-eyed down at Dolores. "I heard a crash—"

"She's dead," said Mr Renner. "What have you done?"

"I didn't—" He clutched the roof's edge, looking like he was going to faint. "I didn't see her. I moved some of the roof tiles around, but I didn't know there was nothing holding them together."

Is he telling the truth? I hadn't even noticed he'd left the rest of the group behind to climb up onto the roof, but I didn't see why he'd have cause to lie. Yet as long as Mrs Renner remained unaccounted for, I'd have to keep her name on the suspect list. If she *had* done it, and I hadn't banished her yet... there was nothing for it. I'd need to get rid of her as soon as possible.

Two of the other construction workers helped levitate Louis down off the roof, since he was shaking too hard to walk in a straight line, let alone climb a ladder. The instant his feet hit the ground, Mr Renner pounced on him and the others, bombarding them with questions.

Drew, meanwhile, was on his phone to someone, probably the police. He hung up a moment later, glancing around at Carey and me. "Can you stay here until the police show up?"

"Sure." I nodded to Carey, who looked pale and scared. Her ghost goggles lay askew, while she still hadn't explained when and why she'd decided to skip school after I'd dropped her off. With the police on the way, I didn't want to add to her worry about having to explain what she'd seen, so I said nothing.

The police showed up within ten minutes. A werewolf officer with blond hair and broad shoulders called a terrified-looking Carey over for questioning, and despite my protests, he wouldn't let me accompany her. Reluctant to end up drawn into Mr Renner's ranting at the builders, I retreated into the back garden and found myself standing in a swamp. The area around the back of the house was so overgrown I hadn't seen how damp the ground was, no doubt due to the river curving around the edge of the house. I backed onto drier ground and used my wand to remove the water from my shoes.

After checking nobody was watching, I turned my back on the house and whispered, "Mart, where are you?"

He appeared an instant later. Despite his propensity for running off and getting up to mischief, he never strayed too far from me. "What now? I was in the middle of a delightful and involved argument with your ghostly intruder."

"Wait, you were talking to Mrs Renner?" I glanced over my shoulder at the now-prominent gap in the roof tiles near where the rat shifter had been standing. "For how long?"

"A few minutes," he said. "I don't know, I didn't set a timer. Why?"

"Because a bunch of roof tiles just fell and killed someone," I said. "Someone who used to be Mrs Renner's mortal enemy."

"Ooh, she was?" he said. "I thought she'd have a few of those."

"It isn't funny," I hissed. "She *died*, Mart."

"So did I, but you don't see me complaining."

I ground my teeth. "What did she have to say to you, then? Were you having a chat about the long-term pros and cons to spending years as a bodiless spirit?"

"No, she wanted to have a whine about all the people who wronged her."

"I see you've found common ground." If she'd been with Mart, maybe she hadn't been responsible for the falling roof tiles, but I knew from experience that ghosts were expert multitaskers when they wanted to be. "Did she say whether her death was an accident or not?"

"No. I wasn't working from a script." He drifted over the swampy ground. "She listed all these people who she wanted to haunt if she could get out of the house."

"Like who?" I asked. "Didn't you take notes?"

"With what?" he said. "I don't have a notebook and pen, in case you've forgotten."

"All right, all right," I said. "It would have helped if she'd given those names when I was talking to her, that's all."

It would also help to have a list of people who'd have a reason to target both her *and* Dolores... except for those who were being questioned by the police right now, that is.

"Maybe she likes me better," Mart said. "She's not thrilled with you being here at the house, and she said she's not going anywhere, whether there's a Reaper around or not."

"That figures," I said. "I wanted to banish her, but if she *was* murdered, someone out there in town is a killer. And now we have another potential murder victim, who might have been killed by the ghost herself. It's a mess."

"You couldn't just take on a simple job, could you?" He shook his head at me. "What about the detective, then? Does he still think I don't exist?"

"He and I came to an understanding, for a wonder," I said. "We did some investigating in the house, but Mrs Renner didn't want to know."

"Oh, really?" he said. "You know, I thought there was something weird about the way he looked at you. He *likes* you."

I frowned. "He has a funny way of showing it if he does. He's just here to get to the bottom of Mrs Renner's death, nothing more. Did she tell you who hired him?"

"No, she didn't. Why not ask him yourself?" He grinned. "Tell you what, buy him a drink or five at the bar next to the inn. That ought to do it."

"No," I said a little too loudly. "We've barely started being civil to each other. Besides, he won't tell me. Confidentiality policies and all that."

I clamped my mouth shut when I spotted the man himself crossing the garden towards me. Mart snickered and made kissing noises, which I studiously ignored. *Honestly.*

"Hey," I said. "Any luck?"

"It's not looking good for Louis," said Drew. "Turns out he and Dolores don't have a pleasant history. She was always hanging out at Mrs Renner's house while the construction was in progress and I gathered they weren't fond of one another."

I arched a brow. "Enough for him to drop a roof on her head and make it look like an accident?"

"I couldn't say." He glanced behind him. "You should take Carey home. Her mum might have heard what happened by now, and she'll be worried about her."

Especially since Carey was supposed to be at school. "All right, but I expect an update later."

His brows rose. "If you like. I'll drop by the inn."

It was only when I'd turned away that I realised I'd implied I *wanted* to see him later. Maybe Mart was rubbing off on me. Things had changed between us so abruptly that I couldn't make heads or tails of it, and Dolores's sudden death didn't help in the slightest.

Besides, I had Carey to worry about. She walked with me out of the house in silence, her expression downcast, and I had no idea how to comfort her. After we'd walked in silence for a few minutes, she turned to me with her eyes brimming over with tears. "I didn't do anything. I swear. I didn't kill her."

"The police didn't give you a hard time, did they?"

She shook her head. "No, but I... I shouldn't have hidden under the table. What if they blame me?"

"They won't," I insisted. "It's poor Louis who's going to take the brunt of this, by the sound of things, but the odds are high that it was an accident. Or Mrs Renner's ghost. Not the ideal scenario, I admit."

"How do you know it might have been her?" she asked. "You didn't see her, did you?"

"No." I wasn't sure how Mart would feel about me telling people he existed. I'd never told anyone since the year or so after his death, and that was a long time ago. It wasn't like she could actually see him, either. But mentioning my brother's ghost would invite in a flood of questions I didn't know how to answer yet.

We reached the inn, where we found Carey's mother

behind the desk in the lobby. She gasped a little when she saw Carey. "What's going on?"

I moved back to let Carey explain. Her mum would be able to give her a level of reassurance I couldn't give her myself, and besides, I was the one who'd dropped her off at school and assumed she'd stay there. The other issue was that I'd originally intended to leave Hawkwood Hollow and go home today, but I couldn't imagine turning my back and leaving this level of chaos behind. Besides, Carey wanted me to stay. Even Drew no longer wanted me gone, as weird as it might seem.

Carey left the lobby and went upstairs, while her mother approached me. Some of the tension inside me unknotted when I saw her expression was filled with concern, not disapproval.

"Sorry about earlier," I said. "I did drop her off outside the academy, but I should have kept a closer eye on her."

"Don't worry about it," she said. "Carey is strong-willed, and she's been having a rough time at school lately. I should have guessed she wouldn't want to be left out while you went back to Mrs Renner's house. None of us could have guessed such a tragic event would take place while she was there."

"I still feel like there's more I could have done." I hadn't managed to find Mrs Renner's killer, if there was one, and now the number of dead bodies had doubled.

"Regardless, I wanted to thank you for taking care of Carey," she said. "Since her father's death, she's had this unending fascination with ghosts, to the extent that it often gets her into trouble. To tell you the truth, I'm relieved she's found someone who can give her guidance."

My stomach squirmed with guilt. I didn't think I'd

done *that* spectacular a job, considering I'd led her head-first into a confrontation with Mrs Renner's ghost and she'd then witnessed another murder. Not that I'd actually known she was there at the time, but still.

"I'll try to keep her out of trouble," I said. "Truth be told, this isn't like any other ghost case I've dealt with. I don't typically run into spirits who were murdered, or believe they were. Nor one who's quite this violent."

At least not with a teenager in tow, anyway.

She nodded. "It's a tricky case, and a pity all around. Carey might have mentioned Mrs Renner was supposed to be staying here at the inn on the day of her death. The weather prevented the construction workers from going in and she really wasn't in a fit state to go wandering around that old house."

"I didn't know the construction workers were supposed to be there." I thought back to the rat shifter's terrified expression when he'd seen poor old Dolores lying dead on the ground. "So she went back there alone… why?"

To prevent Dolores from going to the house and knocking it down while she wasn't there, she'd said, but Dolores herself had claimed not to have been there and the goblin's reports had backed her up.

"I don't know, but she was attached to her home," she said. "There wasn't anything I could do to convince her to stay away while it was under repair."

Hmm. "The construction workers mentioned there might have been sabotage. Of the magical sort, I mean."

"I haven't spoken to the construction workers, so I wouldn't know," she said. "As for sabotage… she certainly made enough enemies. I wonder what that Dolores was doing at her house earlier. It seems a strange time for her to visit."

"That's what I don't get." Even if Mrs Renner had somehow caused her death, why had she been there in the first place?

"Whatever the case, I'm sure the police will get to the bottom of it," she said. "As for you, Maura, you don't have to worry about paying for your room while you stay here. I gather that it might take a few more days to draw out Mrs Renner's ghost and deal with her, what with there being an active investigation on at the house."

"You don't have to let me stay here for free," I protested. "You can take it out of my payment for dealing with the ghost, I don't mind."

"We have the rooms to spare, and you don't cause trouble, dear," she said. "And you've been good to Carey, too."

I looked down, embarrassed. "Not to pry, but I've noticed the town is overrun with ghosts. Has... I mean, has her father's ghost ever been seen?"

"No, he died on a work trip outside of the town," she said. "A freak accident. It hit Carey hard, I think, as she's an only child and she's always been sensitive."

"Did you know about the local ghosts, though?" I asked. "I don't mean to be nosy, but I've lived in quite a few magical communities and there's usually a Reaper assigned to each region who is typically tuned in to everything happening within the area. If there isn't one, then the Reaper Council tends to show up and send their own people in. This place feels abandoned, almost, despite having its own Reaper. It's not typical."

"The Reaper has been retired for a long while." She

lowered her gaze, but not before I caught a flash of emotion in her eyes. "You'll have to ask him if you want to know why."

"I doubt that's a good idea." Given his reaction to my earlier questions, anyway. He wasn't a friendly person and was doubtless as secretive about his past as he was about his reasons for spurning his duty and letting the ghosts of the town's citizens stay here long past their sell-by dates.

Come to think of it, Dolores's ghost might be the next to show up. Not right away—there was often a gap between someone's death and their ghost making an appearance, even without a Reaper in charge of taking people's souls away—but soon. Within the next day. As for whether her ghost would appear at the house or not, though… I doubted Mrs Renner would take kindly to a second ghost moving in, especially her mortal enemy.

Given the little I knew about Dolores, it seemed more likely that her ghost would show up at the retirement home. Even if she wasn't already there, talking to the other resident spirits might be a fruitful line of enquiry if I wanted to find out why Dolores had made her sudden, fateful decision to pay a visit to Mrs Renner's house.

No doubt the staff at the retirement home would be talking to the police right now, but the image of the ghosts flocking around the place filled my mind. What with the recent shock and my fixation on Mrs Renner, I'd forgotten all about the other ghosts for the first time since I'd arrived in town. Except for Mart, of course.

That settled it. After saying goodbye to Carey's mother, I left the hotel and called Mart to my side. "Fancy meeting some of the other ghosts?"

"Which ghosts?" he asked. "I've already met the ones at the inn."

"We're going to the retirement home," I said. "I want to see if any of the ghosts there saw Dolores leave. Or if Dolores herself showed up yet."

He pulled a face. "Why not ask the detective instead?"

"He's busy," I said. "Besides, I don't need to ask his permission."

He snorted. "If you ask me, he's waiting for your permission to ask you out."

"Just where are you getting this from?" I said. "Since when were you so interested in my non-existent love life, anyway?"

"Since the chemistry between you two practically set Mrs Renner's house on fire. It made me need a cold shower, and I'm a ghost."

"You're being ridiculous."

I didn't *like* the detective. We barely knew one another, and he refused to tell me anything about himself. Okay, we hadn't exactly had many chances for a chat outside of the ongoing investigation, but my entire life was overshadowed by the dead. It was part and parcel of being a Reaper.

And to be honest, most of the time, it was easier to stick with the ghosts than attempt to understand the living.

10

I took my time walking back to the retirement home, part of me expecting to see the police gathering there, too. Instead, nobody appeared to be around. Nobody living, anyway. A few ghosts drifted about, and I looked around for a promising target who might be willing to talk to me. The high fence surrounding the building prevented me from seeing inside the back garden, so I didn't know if old Dolores's ghost might be hanging out in the same spot she'd occupied when I'd last spoken to her.

I was about to knock on the front door when the ghost of an old man walked out with a purposeful stride. He turned around to close the door and, since it was already shut, fell through it. He caught his balance, saw me looking, and his expression turned sheepish.

"Sometimes I forget," he said. "You're new here, aren't you?"

"I am," I said. "How'd you know I can see you?"

He couldn't know I was a Reaper, or else he'd have run

for the hills at the very sight of me. Most spirits couldn't tell until I deliberately showed off my talents and started waving around my shadowy magic. Without a scythe, I looked like any other ordinary witch.

"Oh, you have a look about you, know what I mean?" he said. "Were you here to visit someone?"

"Dolores Malone died earlier today," I said. "Have you seen her?"

"Alive or dead?"

"Either," I said. "She died at Mrs Renner's house. Did you see her leave the retirement home?"

"Who?" he said. "Oh, *her.* Nasty woman. Never had a kind word to say to anyone. Whenever we tried to invite her to live here and leave that awful old house behind, she responded with nothing but anger and ingratitude."

"So this has been going on for a while?" I asked. "People asking her to move out of the house?"

"Yes, you'd think we were all after that property for our own use, the way she kept banging on about it," he said. "The truth is, everyone knows it's on its last legs. If her grandson actually fixes it up, he might have a chance of selling it to one of the coven members, but that's assuming he sticks around this time."

So Mr Renner had been here in Hawkwood Hollow before? He'd given me the impression this was his first time here.

"He met his grandmother before her death?" I asked casually. "I thought he'd never been here before."

"He tried to convince her to move out, I heard, but gave up and left town," he said. "This was two years or more back, mind."

"What are you doing?" said a voice.

I spun around. The Reaper of all people stood behind me, arms folded and a scowl on his face. A cigarette hung from his lips, and I eyed it warily in case he threw it at me again. He didn't have his scythe, at least, but why was he looking at me like I'd committed a crime?

"Talking." There was no use denying I'd been speaking to a ghost. "About the recent death of Dolores Malone. Which I suppose you'd know about."

Reapers had a kind of sixth sense which told them when someone in the vicinity had died even when they were nowhere nearby. Mine had faded for the most part—which was frankly a relief, considering life was difficult enough without adding a built-in alarm that alerted you every time someone died—but he must still be able to detect when someone within his region passed away.

He grunted. "Why are you so interested in her death?"

"It happened while I was there," I told him. "Have you seen Dolores's ghost? Can you call her back to speak to me?"

"Certainly *not*." His vehemence made me take a step back, and his cigarette fell from his mouth. "You don't live here. Leave now, if you know what's good for you."

"Whoa." I held up my hands. "I'm not doing anything wrong. You're the one who accosted me. If you won't enlighten me on what your issue is, please go and bother someone else."

I pointedly turned away, but of course the ghost of the old man was long gone. He might not have known about my Reaper powers, but he must have recognised the old retired Reaper and scarpered.

"I have a problem with nosy good-for-nothing outsiders telling me how to do my job," he growled.

"You're *not* doing your job. That's the point." I decided not to press the issue, and with the ghost gone, there was little point in me staying here. Of all the times for him to show an interest in the citizen's lives—or deaths—he had to pick now. Strange, really, given his apparent reluctance to put that scythe of his to the proper use.

I walked away, feeling the Reaper glaring at me until I turned the street corner and he was lost to sight. Exhaling a relieved breath, I startled when I spotted someone else entirely on the other side of the road, heading for the nursing home.

Mr Renner. What was he doing here? It wasn't like he had any other retired grandparents to visit. None that I'd known about, anyway. It was weird to see him so soon after the ghost of the old man had mentioned this wasn't his first visit here to Hawkwood Hollow, too, but I couldn't exactly stop and speak to him with the Reaper still glaring daggers at me, so I left him to it and made my way back to the Riverside Inn.

Nobody was around when I entered the lobby. I could hear chatter from the restaurant, but I wasn't really in the mood for socialising. Carey must still be in her room, and she probably didn't want to be disturbed after her earlier scare. I explored the lower floor of the inn instead, finding an unoccupied games room through a door adjoining the lobby.

"Hey, I like this game." Mart appeared hovering by the games table in the corner. "It's one I can actually play."

He didn't have much firepower as a ghost, but he could use simple telekinesis well enough to pick up a floating ball and levitate it around the board. He always beat me, too. Sometimes I let him win, just to let him have his small amusements.

"Want a game?" I pulled out my wand and levitated the ball into the air.

"Sure." He held up his hands and mimicked holding a wand, and the game began.

Playing an intense competition with Mart did make me feel better. Marginally, anyway. I'd just lost my third game in a row when Mart suddenly looked up, exclaimed, and vanished, the ball dropping to the floor.

I turned around and saw Detective Drew was watching me from beside the half-open door to the lobby. "What are you doing here?"

"Are you playing against yourself?" His gaze followed the ball as it rolled to a stop.

"Yes." I drew myself upright. "Got a problem with that? I had some spare time and nothing else to do."

Thanks to the Reaper. Not that I really had much in the way of hobbies, anyway. I'd been cut off from the magical world for too long to keep up with recent events and gossip, and the ghosts made it difficult to socialise even in the normal world. The one time I'd joined a local hiking club, I'd been pursued halfway across the Yorkshire moors by a wandering spirit. Even in the middle of nowhere, the dead managed to hound me.

"I'm surprised you didn't go back to Mrs Renner's house after dropping Carey at home," he said.

"Didn't seem appropriate with the police around," I said. "Since, you know, I'm not supposed to be involved with the investigation."

"The police have left the house by now," he said. "The

construction crew have, too. You asked for an update, so I brought one."

So I had. Though I'd hoped to find out more from Dolores's friends about her presence at the house, and even Drew might be hard-pressed to get the Reaper to tell him what he was doing lurking around the retirement home.

Mart reappeared beside me. "Ask him out. You know you want to."

I ignored him. "What's the verdict? Was Dolores's death an accident?"

"I was hoping you could ask the ghost that."

He wanted *me* to speak to the ghost? For the second time in a day? "I thought the house was off-limits."

"Not in the slightest," he said. "Want to go there now?"

Mart snickered. "He should have just asked you to see a movie with him, but I guess he already gets your vibe."

I closed my eyes, wishing I could tune him out, and said, "I can't really take Carey with me again, and I feel bad for leaving her out of it."

Surprise flashed in his eyes. "I thought you were here to get rid of Mrs Renner's ghost, whether you had company or not. Why can't you bring her with you?"

"Because I'm almost certain Mrs Renner didn't die of natural causes, and now a second person is dead. If it turns out she *did* do it, then I don't know what she'll do when we show up there again."

She'd already tried to crush a woman underneath a sofa and possibly killed another one with fallen roof tiles. It was difficult not to wonder if things would have turned out differently for all of us if I'd just banished her on my first time in the house.

"Seems like a good argument for making another trip to the house before the construction workers get back," he said. "What do you think?"

"All right." I picked up the ball and put it back on the game table. "I'll see what I can do."

If nothing else, I might be able to talk to her again. She'd spoken to Mart earlier, which ought to prove she was open to conversation. It bothered me—a lot—that she might have murdered someone on her property, but the only way to know what Dolores had been doing there was to ask the woman herself.

"Oh, you're just going to leave me here?" Mart yelled behind me.

I gave him an eye-roll and followed Drew before those sharp eyes of his noticed I was communicating with someone invisible. The sun had begun to sink below the buildings, although we still had a few hours left until it got fully dark. I walked alongside Drew, surprised to find myself relieved to have his company to go back to Mrs Renner's house. Even though I'd really prefer not to expose my Reaper talents in front of him. I still didn't know what *he* was, and I wanted… I didn't know what I wanted. A normal night.

Even if it did involve visiting a haunted house. Again.

The police and the construction workers had left Mrs Renner's house, as Drew had said, leaving the place deserted. I assumed Mr Renner was back at the inn with his wife, though I hadn't seen them come in. Maybe they'd returned while Mart and I had been messing around in the games room.

"What happened after I left?" I asked Drew.

"The police interrogated the construction crew, but

didn't come to any conclusions," he said. "Mr Renner wanted to press charges against Louis, but there's no evidence to show he was responsible for the roof tiles falling off."

Hmm. "Maybe he wasn't. It's hard to tell what's the ghost's fault and what isn't."

Talking to her again would be a good place to start. The two of us entered the house using the key under the porch and stepped into the dark hallway. Drew turned on the light, closing the door behind us.

"Mrs Renner?" I called out. "We're here to talk to you."

I cast Drew a sideways look, half expecting his expression to change, but he looked serious. He really did believe me, and he trusted me to do this. With a new resolve, I headed down the hallway towards the stairs.

A sudden, roaring wind rattled through the house, blowing open every door until they rattled in their frames.

"Get out!" yelled Mrs Renner's ghost.

Not again. "We just want to talk to you!"

"Where is she?" Drew asked.

"I think she might be upstairs again." Not that I could tell, with her creepy voice echoing throughout the whole house. "Mrs Renner, we're just here to ask you a question."

"Get out!" Her words were accompanied by another blast of air, followed by an alarming crash from outside.

Dread clutched at me as I turned my back and ran for the door, crossing my fingers that nobody had been in the line of fire this time around. "Where'd that come from?"

"There." Drew halted in the dark garden and pointed to the ground beneath one of the boarded-up windows, where the wooden boards had fallen out and scattered onto the grass. "It's okay—nobody is here but us."

"And she doesn't want us here." She hadn't yelled at me when I'd spoken to her alone. In fact, come to think of it, she'd only screamed at me to get out of the house when the detective had been there. "It's you she's yelling at, isn't it?"

She didn't want the detective here. But why?

"I don't know, I can't hear her," he said. "What's she saying?"

"Just telling us to get out," I said. "I've only heard her yell like that when you've been around. Not when I came here alone, or when Mr Renner and the construction workers showed up. She told me to go away, but she didn't scream and start slamming doors the way she did then."

"I didn't think she wanted *any* of us here," he said.

She talked to me when I came here alone. Not that I was keen to start another argument now he was finally on my side.

"We'd better close those doors, anyway." I shut the front door firmly, a new plan forming in my mind.

If I wanted to get any answers out of her, I had to come back on my own later. Without the detective.

———

Drew insisted on walking me home, and we parted ways outside the inn. "Are you sure you don't want company for tonight? You've had a long day."

Heat crept up my neck, and I found myself glad Mart

had opted to leave us alone for once. "Uh. I was going to eat at the restaurant—"

The sound of a crash from inside the building made me jump. Drew peered over my shoulder through the glass doors. "Doesn't look like anyone's hurt, don't worry."

"Guess I'm a little jumpy," I said. "Because of the ghost. I'll see what that was."

Not my smoothest exit, but the instant I walked into the lobby, I forgot all about worrying over Drew's intentions. Inside the restaurant, someone had knocked an entire tray of drinks over. Carey's mother hurried over to the mess, clearing it up with a wave of her wand.

"Hey." I walked through the adjoining door into the restaurant. "What's going on?"

"Oh—Maura," she said in distracted tones. "Hayley never showed up for work, and we're overrun here."

"Oh, no." I knew they didn't have that many staff, and Allie seemed to do most of the work herself. "Where's Carey?"

"She'll have to take over on the front desk while I'm in here, but I hate leaving her alone." She put her wand away, her expression frazzled.

"Is there anything I can do to help?" I might not have a ton of experience, but I didn't want to leave the two of them to shoulder the burden alone. "I've worked as a receptionist before. I can help Carey out. Or she can help me out. One or the other."

"Is that okay?" she asked. "I wouldn't pressure you, but there are so few of us as it is... hopefully Hayley is just running late, but she hasn't called me. It's not like her."

"Don't worry about it," I said. "I'm sure Carey can tell me where everything is."

"Grab something to eat first," she said. "And—oh, was that the detective outside?"

I spun on the spot, but Drew had vanished. So much for his hints about keeping me company. I hadn't the time to ponder on his disappearance, so I grabbed a quick dinner and then met Carey in the reception area.

"Hey," I said. "Apparently, I'm your assistant now."

"Did Hayley never show up?" A worried frown appeared on her face. "It's weird. I don't think she's taken a day off since she started working here last year."

"There aren't any other staff?" I asked. "Isn't it stressful?"

"We can handle it," she said. "I know where everything is in the restaurant, but Mum says I'm too young to sell alcoholic drinks at the bar. We have another girl who works in the bar part-time, but she's not supposed to be in today."

"Lucky I'm here, then." *I hope.* My job history consisted a lot of short stints in various places, most of which had ended in ghost-related disasters. At least Carey already knew of my propensity for attracting wayward spirits so it wouldn't turn into an unwanted surprise.

"Are you sure you want to help?" she said. "You're already dealing with the ghost."

"I do have experience as a receptionist in a hotel," I said. "Back in the normal world. Anyway, I'm not sure I've done that much ghost-hunting since I showed up."

"You worked in the normal world?" she asked. "I thought you were always a ghost hunter."

"Yeah... not quite." I decided not to mention all my failed attempts to live a normal life, inside the magical world and outside of it. "I moved around a lot. I've tried lots of different jobs. Nothing quite stuck."

Or to be more precise, *I* didn't stick anywhere. Ever since I'd left home, I'd been adrift, unable to settle, inside the magical world or otherwise. Now, though, I had to admit I felt like I'd been here in Hawkwood Hollow longer than a couple of days. The ghosts were a nuisance, but at least they were a fixture, not causing endless disruption. With one obvious exception.

"Oh." She bit her lip. "Um, you went back to the house again, didn't you?"

"Not for long," I said. "The detective told me the police finally left, so I went back to talk to Mrs Renner's ghost to see if I could get an idea of what happened to Dolores. She yelled at us and pretty much pushed us out of the house without letting us get any further than the hall. To tell you the truth, I think it's the detective she doesn't want there."

"Why?" she asked.

"I don't know, she wouldn't say." I hovered on the balls of my feet, feeling uneasy. "You'd think she'd want him to solve her murder. Unless it was me she was yelling at, but she seemed willing to talk to me the last time I went to speak to her alone. I guess we'll have to go back tomorrow."

Or tonight, but I'd already volunteered to help Carey and her mother out at the inn. I mentally pushed back my deadline to leave town another couple of days and returned my attention to the task at hand. It was nice to have something to do with my evening which didn't involve hanging out with my brother. Mart and I had spent countless nights watching old *Doctor Who* episodes or arguing about Sky Hopper, which, while enjoyable, got old after a while.

We worked until the restaurant closed for the night and most of the guests had returned to their rooms, at which pointed Allie reappeared and insisted that Carey go to bed.

"You should turn in for the night, too," she said to me. "Not that I'm trying to act like your parent or anything. It's a habit."

There was an unspoken question in her words, one I knew would come up at some point.

"My parents aren't around," I admitted. "It's been a while since anyone's told me to go to bed."

"Okay, just let me know if it bothers you." She stepped in behind the reception desk, while Carey made for the stairs and waved goodnight to her.

I was about to follow her when I spotted Mr Renner coming back downstairs. Without noticing me, he crossed the lobby to the doors. Was he going back to the house? Now? It was dark outside, and nobody would be around... which seemed awfully suspicious to me.

I slipped out from behind the desk and headed for the door myself, casting a concealment charm on myself to avoid drawing his attention. Mr Renner didn't look back, but he crossed the bridge and then turned to walk in the opposite direction to his grandmother's house. I trod behind him, wondering where on earth he was going. Then his route turned uphill towards the town cemetery, and I knew before he reached the cottage that he was heading up to the Reaper's house.

I stopped mid-step. Even though I'd used a spell to conceal myself, Reapers had ways of detecting living people no matter what kind of magic they'd used. Ghosts, on the other hand…

"Mart," I whispered. "I need your help."

"Yes?" He appeared at my side. "I thought you were on a date with that detective of yours."

"Mr Renner is going to visit the Reaper," I said. "I'd follow him, but I'm pretty sure he's less likely to spot you than he is me."

"So you want me to take your place?" he said. "You do realise the Reaper can see *me* as well as he can see you, don't you?"

"Yes, but a living person trespassing would draw too much attention," I said. "There are so many ghosts here, they're probably background noise to him now. He won't know you're spying on him. Please?"

He grumbled under his breath. "You'll owe me for this."

"You can stand under my shower for an hour and I'll pay the water bill," I said. "Go on, quickly, before it's too late."

I ducked down as a face appeared in the window of the Reaper's cottage. Mr Renner. *What is he doing? Asking for the Reaper's help with the ghost?* Admittedly, I should have got rid of her myself by now, but I'd have thought Mr Renner might have wanted to clear up the murder issue first. Not to mention the question of the second victim's death. Had the Reaper seen *her* ghost? Now was most definitely not the time to ask, so I turned away and left Mart to do his spying.

I'd have to get answers tomorrow instead.

11

I woke up the following morning in better spirits than I had the right to be in, considering I'd come no closer to solving the murder and was more confused than ever about Mrs Renner's behaviour. If I'd guessed right and she didn't want the detective in her house, then I was at a loss to guess why. If she was so certain she'd been murdered, you'd think she'd want someone around with the authority to arrest her murderer. Even if he couldn't actually see her and had to depend on someone else's testimony.

Which, incidentally, was why the word of a ghost had less sway than you'd think among the paranormal law enforcement. Too few people could communicate with spirits for them to be considered reliable witnesses.

Speaking of ghosts, Mart had yet to show his face even after I'd conjured some of my clothes from home, showered and dressed. I'd need to check in with him for a report on whether he'd found out why Mr Renner was meeting with the Reaper, but I'd already overslept, so I went downstairs once I'd finished dressing.

It was the weekend, so the breakfast buffet was even quieter than usual. Mr Renner was nowhere to be seen, but I caught sight of Carey's mother working at the bar and gave her a wave and smile. I loaded up my plate and joined Carey at a table where she sat with her familiar, Casper.

"Hey." On the table next to her lay her ghost goggles and her recording device, while an earbud dangled from one ear. "I'm watching the footage from yesterday."

"Oh?" I dug into my meal, though my appetite dulled at the memory of poor Dolores's death. "Did you get any decent footage of the ghost?"

"Check it out." She held up the miniature camera so I could see better, and the fuzzy, blurred image of a floating plank of wood came into view. "I'm trying to see if I managed to record her speaking."

"Maybe hold off on uploading it to your blog until the ghost is gone, in case she objects to it," I suggested, picking up a piece of toast. "Is Mr Renner around?"

Her gaze flickered around the restaurant. "I haven't seen him today. Mum said he went out last night."

To see the Reaper. Not that that necessarily meant anything nefarious. For all I knew, he'd asked the Reaper to get rid of his grandmother's ghost since I'd failed to do so myself. Mart's absence made me uneasy, but as I wasn't yet ready to share him with the others, I'd have to look for him later. I dug into my meal instead while Carey showed me some of her footage, until Allie walked over to join us.

"Thanks for helping out last night," said Carey's mother. "It's appreciated. Sorry about the short notice."

"Glad I could help," I said. "It's nice to be able to do something useful."

I meant it, too. She and Carey were the nicest people I'd met in a while, and it was a shame the town wasn't more popular with tourists. Maybe there was a way I could take some of the load off them. With so few staff, one absence could cause a major problem.

She smiled. "Hayley called me and let me know she'll be back in tonight, but I'll definitely consider hiring someone else to step in. We should be fine today, though."

"Good, because I may have to borrow Carey." I caught her eye. "Want to go back to the house?"

"Sure!" The way her expression brightened made me glad I hadn't opted to get rid of the ghost last night after all. "Will Mr Renner be there, do you know?"

"That man." Her mother tutted and shook her head. "I haven't seen him today, but he returned late last night and woke me up by hammering on the bell at the reception desk. I did tell him the desk is closed at midnight, but he insisted on demanding new bedcovers in his room. Something about his wife being allergic to the material, I've no idea. Frankly, I'll be glad when they're gone, regardless of the money they bring in."

Yet another reason for me to go straight to Mrs Renner's house—without the detective this time. Since it was the weekend, Carey would be able to go with me without skipping school, which was good news for all of us. It surprised me how quickly I'd fallen into a routine, and at this point, I couldn't imagine turning back until I'd solved this case and banished Mrs Renner's ghost.

"He's certainly got a temper," I remarked. "Did he say where he went last night?"

"Back to the house, I assume," said Allie.

"Pity the ghost didn't show up," Carey put in.

Her mother tutted. "He mentioned that. Said the builders were making excuses for their own incompetence by blaming it on a ghost."

"Did he?" I frowned. "Did he mention old Dolores, or drop any hints about who he thinks might have killed her?"

"Hints?" she echoed. "Not that I heard. He was mostly grumbling about the builders and his grandmother's attachment to the house."

"Is he really that desperate to have the place, then?" I asked. "I thought he worked elsewhere."

"I got the impression he wanted to sell the place, not live in it."

"I doubt anyone will be disappointed, given how he's treated everyone in town so far." I rose to my feet. "Whether he's at the house or not, I think today's the day. I'm going to talk to Mrs Renner, and if I can't gain her cooperation… she has to go."

Carey grabbed her ghost goggles and put them back on her head. They might look vaguely ridiculous, but from what I'd seen, the camera did work even if the goggles themselves didn't. Not that I was keen to drag her into danger with me again. One person had already died on the property—not counting old Mrs Renner herself.

"Don't forget to grab your coat," Allie told Carey, who rolled her eyes at her mother and pulled out her wand. With a flick, her coat appeared in her hands and she shrugged into it. Casper bounded off the table and Carey gave him a stroke, then her familiar walked away through the restaurant.

After waving goodbye to Allie, the two of us set off for Mrs Renner's house once again.

"I usually help out at the restaurant at the weekend," Carey admitted. "But I don't want to miss out on this."

"I can't say anything else I've tried this week has gone according to plan," I admitted, "and to be honest, I'd like to know more about what Mr Renner is doing here. He's been to the town before."

"He has?" she said.

"According to a ghost I met at the retirement home," I said. "Come to think of it, Mr Renner was heading that way last time I saw him, so perhaps that's why the Reaper was there."

"Wait, you saw the *Reaper* at the retirement home?" Her eyes rounded. "Was he looking for Dolores's ghost?"

"Maybe." Not that he'd admitted anything to me. "He wouldn't tell me why he was there, but last night, I saw Mr Renner going to visit the Reaper after dark, too. No idea why, unless the two of them were discussing how to banish his grandmother's ghost."

Her brow furrowed. "Then might the Reaper have already banished her?"

I hadn't thought of that. "I'm not sure. Depends if the Reaper took him up on his offer and went to Mrs Renner's house last night." I skipped over the part where I'd sent Mart to spy on him. I still hadn't seen Mart today, which was odd, but it wasn't unheard of for him to wander off for a while. "I couldn't get too close to the Reaper's house without being spotted, so I had to leave. Reapers have the ability to detect anyone close to them even if they can't be seen."

"Does that mean you do, too?" she asked curiously.

"You're half Reaper, right? I remember you saying that in the interview."

"Yes." I buried my hands in my pockets, reluctant to dig into my history even now. "I make more use out of my witch skills, though. I don't have a scythe or anything. Being a Reaper is a pretty lonely job, so it never appealed to me."

"Is that why Harold is so miserable?" she asked.

"I have no idea, and I doubt he'd tell me if I asked," I said. "I'm more likely to get answers from Mr Renner than him, and that's saying a lot."

We reached Mrs Renner's house and found the door already open, several construction workers milling about. I scanned the front of the house, but thankfully saw no signs of the detective. Nor the Reaper, either.

Louis gave me a wave, smiling nervously. "Hey, there."

"You haven't seen Mr Renner, have you?" I asked.

"He's running errands with his wife, I heard," he said. "No sign of his grandmother either… not that I'm keen to jinx it, given the mess she made yesterday."

"Her ghost hasn't shown up?" She'd yelled at the detective and me last night, but she didn't seem bothered by the construction workers. Why might that be?

"Not that we've seen or heard," he said. "We're used to ignoring strange noises from inside the house, though. Those of us who scare easily left the job ages ago."

That made sense, but he and the others must be seriously dedicated to still be working after either the ghost or the old building had caused a fatal accident. Then again, maybe they were as broke as I was. I mean, if the choice was between spending a night in a haunted house or being kicked out of my apartment, I'd pick the ghost every time.

"Have you made much progress?" I asked.

"For a start, we have to figure out what to do with this extension she had put in a few years ago," he said. "I'd like to tear the whole thing down, but Mr Renner was furious at me for suggesting it."

"Which extension?" I followed his line of sight to the doorway leading to the second half of the hall the back. "Oh—the house used to be smaller?"

"Yes, until we added in the back rooms," he said. "I say 'we'—someone else was in charge of renovations when they were originally put in, of course. There's no upstairs floor at the back there... just the kitchen. That's why the roof at the back is lower."

The same place where those roof tiles had fallen off. And the doorway linking the two halves of the house was where Mrs Renner had died. Now I looked closer, it was the source of why the house looked so patchy and unsteady, as though someone had used a spell to fuse both parts of the building together without checking if the foundations were stable first.

"So that's why there are fewer rooms upstairs than there are down here," I surmised. "How long ago was this extension added?"

"Oh, years ago," he said. "I believe flood-proofing spells were used in the setup, but it's not surprising that the protective spells are failing. They're not supposed to be used for this long."

"Flood-proof?"

He bowed his head. "Yes, for the river, you know... her house is right on top of it."

"That explains why half the garden has turned into a swamp," I remarked, remembering my conversation with Mart while the police had been here yesterday. "Did someone from your team put those spells on the house?"

"No, we didn't," he said. "As I said—this was years ago."

"You mentioned there might be a spell on the house yesterday," I said. "I mean, the sort that might have been intended to cause damage. How can you tell?"

"Wizardly matters aren't my strong point." He cleared his throat. "My team can't take the spell off without potentially causing damage to the house, either."

"Can't you… I don't know, just use a tracking spell to sense what kind of magic was used, then?" I asked. "That seems to me like the obvious choice, if you want to know for certain if there was some kind of sabotage intended."

He glanced nervously up at the ceiling. "Without Mr Renner's permission… I'm loath to say it, but he's been quite uncooperative, and if we use a spell without his say-so, he might well send us packing without pay."

"Is he going to live in this house or not?" I asked. "Either way, he needs it to be in one piece. I don't think there's anything wrong with using a spell to detect if any magical interference is causing some of the trouble. It's not my area of expertise either, but it's worth looking into."

"I suppose you're right," he said. "At first, we thought it might be the ghost moving things around… and then there's the matter of the upstairs floorboards, too, but that's just as likely to be ordinary wear and tear, given the age of the house."

"Yes, but you might as well take a look." Was his reluctance due to not wanting to tick off Mr Renner, or might he have lied about his team's innocence in the damage which had ended in the roof tiles falling off? I wasn't one to point fingers, but something about this whole setup raised my suspicions. "Is there a wizard on your team who can cast a revealing spell?"

"I'll ask." He moved to talk to the rest of his team, while I stepped back to Carey's side.

"Why didn't he think of it earlier?" Carey whispered.

Was it a sign of guilt? Or was he just worried about upsetting Mr Renner? Either might be true, and without any proof either way, I was better off letting him cast the spell and then deciding how to proceed afterwards.

After several minutes of quiet discussion, one of the wizards raised his wand and pointed it at the ceiling. He waved the wand in a series of complex movements, which revealed nothing.

"I don't think it's working," Louis said. "Wait…"

A pattern of vivid lines spread up the wall, across the ceiling and through the entire room. I followed the lines with my vision, eyeing the way they spread and splintered until they covered the entire back section of the house.

"Whoa," I breathed. I might not be accomplished in construction magic, but I knew a destructive spell when I saw one. Someone had cleverly hidden it inside the very walls, and I wouldn't have spotted it at all if not for the revealing spell.

"I'll go and see where it started," said Louis. The rest of the team crowded into the corridor, which seemed like tempting fate with the evidence of the house's instability literally above their heads. "It's only on the extension for the most part… I wonder who built it."

"I couldn't say," said an older wizard with grey hair.

"By all accounts, the woman herself kept trying to take over the job. Maybe she's the one responsible."

"She wanted to knock down her own house? I doubt it." I turned back to Carey and startled at the sight of a transparent greyish figure hovering at the foot of the stairs.

Mrs Renner stood beneath the lines of the spell spreading across the hall ceiling, a scowl on her face.

"Whoa." I half-tripped over my own feet in a hurry to reach her before she vanished. "Mrs Renner. Want to talk now?"

Carey grabbed my arm. "Is she there? Mrs Renner's ghost?"

"She is." I looked the ghostly figure in the eyes. "You probably heard we found a destructive spell someone used on your house which seems designed to make it fall apart. Did that cause your death?"

Her eyes narrowed. "So that's what did it. I always knew there was something amiss, but my eyesight isn't what it used to be. Especially now."

My heart swooped uneasily. *It's true? How did she not notice for years?*

"Who put up the extension?" I asked her. "Did someone put the spell on the house back then, when the extension was built, or was it a recent thing?"

Had Dolores visited her house? It sounded like their history went back years. Mr Renner had visited before-hand, too, as I'd found out yesterday. He certainly had reason to want to turf her out of the house, but without proof, I'd only get myself into trouble if I accused him. And then there was his odd rapport with the Reaper. Maybe he wanted to convince the Reaper to get rid of her ghost to ensure the truth was never exposed. But again… no proof, and the Reaper was unlikely to cooperate, either.

One of Louis's wizard assistants poked his head back into the hallway. "Is she there? Mrs Renner? Did she say who put up the extension?"

"She confirmed the extension has been there for years," I said, "but she doesn't know when the spell was cast. Whatever the case, I don't think it's likely that she put it there herself."

Not if she'd lived here the whole time. I scanned the cracks on the ceiling, looking for a starting point, but they faded out when they reached the front of the house. Carey hovered behind me, goggles on, her mouth pinched in concentration.

"Carey, can you keep an eye on the others?" I asked her. "Let me know if you need me. I'm going to see if I can talk to her alone."

Mrs Renner's ghost hovered in the hall, floating up the stairs a little more with each passing second. I trod as lightly as I dared, one eye on the ceiling, one eye on the ghost. The lines of the destructive spell petered out before they reached the stairs.

"Mrs Renner," I said. "Is there a reason your grandson might be meeting with the Reaper?"

"That scoundrel," she snapped. "I won't leave this house. I won't let him have it."

"Hey—" I took a step forward, and a cold breeze pushed me backwards. In the same instant, Mrs Renner vanished. *Not again.*

I stepped off the stairs, cursing under my breath. What had she meant? Did she think her grandson wanted to banish her out of his desire to sell the house, or might there be something else he wanted to cover up? Asking the Reaper would get me nowhere, but... wait. I still hadn't found Mart.

"Mart?" I called out in a whisper. It wasn't like Mart to vanish, but I didn't blame him for avoiding the house. If I didn't talk to him and find out what had transpired between Mr Renner and the Reaper, though, I'd have no proof but my own suspicions, and they weren't good enough to prove Mr Renner might have been responsible for the damage to his grandmother's house.

Why now, Mart? It would be a fine thing if I finally got rid of him at a time when I desperately needed his expertise.

The front door to the house opened and Mr Renner himself entered the hallway, followed by his wife. At least he'd saved me from looking for him myself, because it was about time I got his side of the story. Without any lies, this time.

12

"Oh, hey, Mr Renner." My cheery tone sounded false to my own ears, not least because I had no adequate explanation for why I was lurking on the stairs now the ghost had gone.

Mr Renner looked me up and down with disdain in his expression. "You again? Have you finally got rid of my grandmother's ghost?"

"I've spoken to her." I sensed from his mood that I'd have to proceed delicately or else he might well kick me out. Especially when he found out about the sabotage spell. "Also, we've exposed a spell in the house's foundations which might have been intended to harm her."

"Is that so?" he said. "Let's see it, then."

He and Claudie entered together, closing the door behind them.

"There." I pointed to the visible lines of the revealing spell criss-crossing the ceiling at the back of the hall. "I think someone may have put a spell on the house when the extension was being constructed."

"They did what?" he said, his face flushing with anger. "Who?"

"Your grandmother didn't say," I said. "She vanished before she could tell me. How long ago was the extension put in? Did you see the people who worked on it?"

"No," he said shortly. "I came here afterwards. Isn't someone going to remove that spell?"

"The construction workers are back there." I pointed through to the kitchen. "I'm not sure if it can be removed without damaging the house… and there's still the matter of who cast it to begin with. If their actions caused your grandmother's death—"

"They'll have to answer to me." He made to march through the hall, only for someone else to walk into the house. A tall, broad-shouldered someone.

Oh, no. The detective was here, too. Which meant the ghost would definitely not make another appearance anytime soon.

"Hey," said Drew. "What's going on here?"

His gaze went to mine, and my heart did a weird skip that I couldn't entirely put down to surprise at his appearance.

Mr Renner accosted him. "*She* says there's a destructive spell on the house."

"The wizards on Louis's team exposed it," I explained, pointing up at the ceiling. "It's been there a while. Possibly since the extension was put in, years ago."

"You're saying the spell was cast years ago?" said Claudie. "If that's the case, how can it be responsible for her death? She lived in this house for fifty years or more, didn't she, Henry?"

"That's right." Mr Renner turned on me with a frown. "Did my grandmother tell you that herself?"

"No, the construction workers did."

"Then someone here is being less than truthful." His gaze went from me to Drew, and then to the group of construction workers who'd realised he was there and drifted out of the kitchen into the hallway to meet him.

Does that mean you're going to confess to meeting with the Reaper? I managed to hold back that comment… just.

"The spell doesn't have to be recent to cause damage," Louis told him. "However, if it turns out to be the cause of the trouble, then we will have to halt all construction work until we can determine if it's safe to remain in the house. Especially with the recent spiritual disturbances."

"I thought that's why you were here," Mr Renner said to me. "You and the girl, too. Where is she?"

Carey popped her head out of the kitchen. "In here. The spell's all over the house, and Maura was going to ask the ghost if she knew who put it there."

Mr Renner scowled at her. "Then what are you doing back here?"

Carey's face flushed. "Um. I can't see ghosts… not without my goggles, anyway."

"Hold on," Drew said.

Mr Renner cut through his words. "Is this a joke? What kind of ghost hunter are you?"

Carey's red cheeks turned even redder, and a wave of anger washed over me.

"Look," I cut in. "The ghost is a witness to two deaths, potentially. And she's the only one of us who was here when the extension was put in. If you want her to show up and give you answers, pointing fingers and being rude to my assistant isn't the best way to go about it."

I wanted to say several less polite things to Mr Renner on top of that, but I managed to hold my tongue. He seemed entirely too keen for us to get rid of the only other witness, and besides, he had no right to be so rude to Carey. Yet the look of gratitude Carey gave me for defending her didn't quell my growing dread when Mr Renner's anger focused on me.

"I could hardly care less about what a ghost has to say," he said. "And I'm inclined to think you and the little schoolgirl are here to get your hands on my grandmother's inheritance instead."

A little gasp escaped Carey, and several tears slid down her cheeks.

My temper snapped. "I thought that's why you hired the Reaper. So he could get rid of her ghost and leave you to sell all her possessions without her getting in the way."

His furious gaze burned through me. "Yes, I did speak to the Reaper yesterday. As it happens, he told me a few interesting things about you… and your brother."

It was suddenly hard to breathe. "How did you—?"

"You don't think I'd let an amateur ghost hunter and a child walk onto my property without looking you up?" he said. "Especially an ex-Reaper?"

I saw Drew move in the corner of my eye, but I didn't look directly at him. I couldn't. *He knows what I am.*

"That is none of your business." My voice shook a little despite my efforts to keep it steady. "Did the Reaper refuse to help you out, then? Or were you hoping he'd get rid of the proof that you already knew about the spell, because you came here to hassle your grandmother to leave this house a couple of years back?"

Carey's mouth fell open, while several gasps came from the direction of the construction workers. This wasn't how I'd imagined it going at all. Mostly because I hadn't planned for my past to return to haunt me at a time like this. I'd really thought I was safe here.

Mr Renner took a threatening step towards me, his wand in his hand. "If I were you, I'd leave this house before I have you arrested."

"Henry, stop it!" Claudie said.

"That won't be necessary," Drew interjected. "I'll escort her out. The girl, too."

Shame heated my cheeks, but I kept my head held high as I walked to the door with Carey trailing behind me. Silent tears continued to fall down her cheeks, and it took great effort for me to resist turning around and giving Mr Renner a tongue-lashing for upsetting her.

"Evil man," I muttered under my breath. "If you ask me, he *did* have his grandmother bumped off."

"I wouldn't advise you to suggest that within hearing distance of him." Drew's disapproving tone made me wilt on the spot. On top of everything else I'd managed to ruin in the last few minutes, I'd accidentally sent our rapport back to square one. "Is there really a spell on the house?"

"Why would I lie about something like that?" Hurt bled into my tone despite my best efforts. "One of Louis's people used a revealing charm which exposed a spell in the extension on the house, and I find it hard to believe that Mr Renner didn't notice when he visited his grandmother two years ago."

Carey glanced at me, wiping her eyes. "She's right."

"How do you know he visited here two years ago?" The suspicion in his tone shouldn't have hurt as much as it did.

"A ghost told me," I said. "At the retirement home. If Mr Renner came here in the past, then it's not too much of a stretch to wonder if he did the same back when the extension was put in."

"Even if it is true, Mr Renner would still have been a teenager when the extension was put in," he said. "According to my research, the extension was built more than a decade ago. I doubt Mrs Renner's grandson was the person who used a slow-acting destructive spell in a long-term plan to get his grandmother's property."

Oh. I should have thought of that. "He's not exactly acting in an innocent manner. If he really cared for his grandmother, he'd want to get justice for her death. And what about poor Dolores?"

"Perhaps he doesn't trust his grandmother's ghost to tell the truth."

Since I'd had the same thought myself once or twice, I had no argument for that. "I thought you wanted justice, too. Or at least closure." I still hadn't the faintest clue what he could possibly get out of solving this case. If I was in his position, I'd have backed off as soon as Mr Renner arrived in town at the very latest.

"There's definitely a spell on the house," said Carey. "Did Mrs Renner tell you who did it?"

"No," I said. "She *did* call her grandson a scoundrel and said she wouldn't let him have the house. Make of that what you will."

"I'll go and deal with him myself," Drew said. "See if I

can get some sense out of him. Both of you—go back to the inn."

"What makes you think he's likely to listen to you?" A warning voice inside my head urged me to let it drop, but I couldn't forget he'd heard every word Mr Renner had said about my Reaper history. Now I'd been kicked out the house, my excuses to stay here in town had evaporated, yet I didn't want to leave without getting some kind of closure. "Look, I saw Mr Renner meeting with the Reaper. Twice. Doesn't that merit another questioning?"

"Not when the Reaper is the only citizen of the town with the ability to banish a powerful spirit like her," he said. "It's understandable that he'd want to get a second option."

Heat crept up my neck. "So you'd rather I banished her ghost without letting you complete your questioning? You might have told me, so I didn't have to waste my time."

A grimace tugged at his mouth. "I'm referring to what I thought *his* reasoning might be, not mine."

"Good to know." I turned to Carey. "Want to head back home? I'll join you in a minute."

"Where are you going first?" She looked between us, a worried frown on her face.

"To the police," I said. "Someone ought to tell them about the destructive spell on the house. Who knows, maybe then they'll open the case again."

Drew gave me a funny look as though wondering what I had to gain from that. In truth, I had no idea, only that I had zero desire to see anyone else in that house end up hurt. If someone in the house *was* involved in her death, then the police would be able to do a better job of probing them than me.

I looked to Carey, but her head was bowed, her cheeks flushed. Something was bothering her. "What is it?"

Carey shuffled her feet, looking up at Drew. "Tell her. It's only fair."

Drew looked at me. "I'm the chief of police here in Hawkwood Hollow. That's why I was at the house."

My mouth fell open. "What? You aren't wearing a badge."

"I'm off-duty," he said in apologetic tones. "Like I was when we first met. There never seemed an appropriate time to tell you."

I forgot all about Mr Renner. "You're... you're the chief of police?"

"I am." He drew in a breath, looking a little embarrassed. "I'm in charge of Mrs Renner's case, but keeping the investigation open was my own idea. Nobody else has come forward with information and the others think I'm wasting my time, but it's my choice."

No wonder he'd pretty much taken charge when the police had shown up yesterday and nobody had raised a fuss. I'd been too fixated on the aftermath and on talking to Mart to really notice.

Mart. Now I had no allies left other than him, and I hadn't seen him since I'd sent him to spy on Mr Renner and the Reaper last night. Mr Renner might not have been able to see him... but the Reaper could.

"So you thought it would be amusing not to tell me who you really were?" I said to Drew.

"Don't blame Carey," Drew said. "She didn't want to get into trouble."

"I don't blame her, I blame you."

He winced. "I'm sorry, but we met under the worst

circumstances, and if I'd been on duty, I'd have had to kick you out of the house there and then."

"You pretty much did that anyway." Irritation spiked inside me. "Is that why you wanted me on your side as soon as you found out I could find out information you couldn't get yourself?"

"No, of course not," he said. "I needed to learn more about Mrs Renner's death, yes, and I hoped if I went with you, she'd show her face."

"Not if she kept telling you to get out." I shook my head. "No wonder she objected to you being in the house, if you're the chief of police and she didn't actually hire you to investigate her murder."

Whatever the case, I could say goodbye to ever being allowed back into that house again. Or the town in general, at this rate.

Drew turned to Carey. "Can you run along home? I need to talk to Maura, but we won't be long," he said.

"No." I didn't meet his eyes. "We won't. I'll see you soon."

Or not.

Carey gave me an apologetic look, then headed back down the road towards the inn, while I turned to face Drew. "Are you kicking me out of town?"

He looked startled. "If I had the authority to kick people out of town for entering abandoned property and accusing unpleasant residents of a crime, half our population would be gone."

I had no idea if he was being serious or not. "I'm not a resident, as you already pointed out. And as you may have gathered, I'm not exactly on good terms with the other Reapers."

He didn't say anything, but I didn't dare meet his eyes in case I saw… I didn't know what I expected to see. Pity, maybe. "I know you aren't."

"You already knew?" I'd suspected, really, since Mr Renner had mentioned the subject. It was in line with how my luck was going today. "I suppose it's your job to research all your suspects."

It seemed Mr Renner wasn't the only person who'd poked into my history, and while I hadn't wanted him to know about Mart, that was the least of what he might have found out.

When he didn't speak, I raised my head. "So you know my twin brother died," I said. "You know I got kicked out of my coven and then gave up being a Reaper. And I suppose *you* think it's all my fault, too."

"No," he said. "I didn't—"

"You don't have to pity me." I looked away. "I had quite enough of that when I was at home—which is why I left and haven't settled anywhere since."

I might as well lay out all my secrets on the table. Now that I knew for sure that I wasn't sticking around here, there was no point in hiding the truth. If he didn't already know it all.

"Maura…" He moved, his hand outstretched as though he'd intended to take my arm and then thought better of it.

"Tell Carey and her mother I'm sorry," I said.

Then I turned my back and walked away. I waited to make sure he wasn't going to follow me before calling for my brother's ghost.

"Mart," I said. "We're leaving."

No response came. Even the ghost of my brother had

abandoned me. I was committed to my path now, so I kept walking, unable to believe things had gone so badly wrong, so fast.

Drew had lied to me about who he was, and I couldn't say I knew why. His excuses were feeble at best, and it left me feeling more confused and wrong-footed than I had the right to. Sure, we might not have met under the best of circumstances, but he might at least have enlightened me on the truth at any point in the last few days. But he'd continued to play me for a fool and lead me along.

I'd about had it with people hiding the truth. Reapers included.

I was halfway up the hill leading out of town when the fog cleared enough for me to see the fields spreading out around the town. Yet even now, Mart still hadn't come back. I'd assumed he'd left me behind, but maybe… maybe he was in trouble. Because I'd sent him to spy on old Harold and Mr Renner at the Reaper's cottage.

What if the old man had done something to Mart? As the Reaper, he was one of few people who *could* harm a ghost… or banish him. Mart might be annoying, but he was my only remaining friend. I had to make sure he was okay.

There was nobody I wanted to visit *less* than the guy who'd been at least partly responsible for my current dilemma, but if he'd done something to my brother's ghost, he'd have to answer to me, and it wouldn't be pretty.

At least it gave me something to concentrate on that wasn't my major screwup or my humiliation at being fooled by the police chief into thinking he was an amateur private detective.

I was probably going to regret this, but I couldn't bring myself to care. I marched back downhill and through the town without stopping to look at anyone, living or dead. I only slowed when I reached the graveyard beside the hill where the Reaper's house stood.

I didn't bother to use a spell to hide myself this time as I reached the house and halted outside. My brother looked at me from behind the window of the Reaper's house, his eyes wide with fear. *I should have known.*

13

Mart's eyes widened and his mouth moved as he spotted me through the window. Whatever he was saying, I couldn't hear, but I'd bet it was as complimentary as my own opinion on the Reaper's nerve at locking my brother's ghost in his house.

I marched up to the door and rapped my knuckles on the wooden surface. "Hey! Open up."

"Go away!" the Reaper yelled back.

"Not likely." I pulled out my wand. "Let my brother go, or I'll blast the door off its hinges."

He wrenched the door open and glared at me. "Thought you were leaving town."

His Reaper senses were on point, it seemed, despite his long retirement. "Not without my brother, I'm not."

He popped a cigarette into his mouth and took a drag. "You know it's against the law to bind a ghost to yourself using your Reaper abilities, don't you?"

I folded my arms. "Only as illegal as locking a ghost in

your house and using your scythe as an ornament. Let him go."

His scowl didn't budge. "You shouldn't have come to Hawkwood Hollow. We don't need any more Reapers here."

"I'm not one," I said. "And I'm not leaving without my brother. You're the one who told Mr Renner my history, so you know I can't possibly be here on behalf of the Reaper Council."

He grunted. "I don't know everything about you. You're a menace and need to be kicked out as soon as possible."

"You flatter me." I peered over his shoulder, seeing Mart hovering in the living room doorway. "What did you do to him?"

"I still have some of my Reaper talents left," he said. "What did *you* do, bind him to you at the moment of his death?"

"That's none of your business." My voice was brittle, my temper fraying at the edges.

"It is if you want him back," he growled. "It's not right, trapping souls in this realm."

"He isn't trapped anywhere except your house," I pointed out. "He can leave at any time."

But he was right, in a way. In order for Mart to move onto the afterlife, I had to let him go. And I hadn't been able to do it in the end. He was a Reaper, like me, and I'd thought we'd live forever.

Instead, he'd died while we'd both been on a stakeout mission chasing a Reaper gone bad, and our target had got the upper hand. Before I'd been able to stop him, he'd used his scythe to sever Mart's soul. I'd done the only thing I could think of, and I'd used my own Reaper powers to bind his soul to mine, keeping him here in this realm. In the process, I'd turned my back on the Reapers' laws and I'd known I could expect no mercy from the Council. All I could do was run.

And I hadn't stopped running since.

His expression softened imperceptibly, as though he'd guessed the direction of my thoughts. Maybe he had, but he was the last person I wanted pity from. On the other hand, if that's what it took to get Mart back and avoid a potential confrontation with the Reaper Council, so be it.

"Fine," said the Reaper. "If it means that much to you, take him with you."

He stepped aside with a gesture towards the cluttered room on his right-hand side. At once, Mart shot out of the room and crashed into me so hard that it felt like a bucket of ice-water had upended over my head. I shuddered and coughed, backing onto the doorstep. "Ow."

"Never again." Mart flew past me, retreating as far from the Reaper's cottage as possible. "Never."

"I'm sorry, Mart." I looked back at the Reaper. "Thanks for freeing him, but that doesn't make us even."

He grunted. "You don't need to tell me you're here for another reason, and you aren't going to leave until you get your way."

"I'm not here to bring the council after you, though you deserve it," I said. "I'm here to help a friend and solve a murder. Which is why I'd like you to tell me what you and Mr Renner were chatting about when he visited your cottage."

His mouth flattened. "That's none of your concern."

"It is if you were talking about Mrs Renner's

murder," I said. "Her grandson isn't acting like an innocent man, and years ago, someone put a spell on his grandmother's house which led to its collapse. I'm not saying he's the definite culprit, but I could use some direction."

"There were two victims, correct?" he said.

"There were, but I couldn't find the second one's ghost." Though I hadn't looked very hard. I'd been too fixated on Mr Renner and that blasted house. "Besides, can you blame me for getting suspicious? You're the one person who *could* get rid of Mrs Renner's ghost, and instead I found you meeting with her living grandson at the place where the second victim came from, during the police investigation."

"Fine," he said. "Henry Renner wanted to ask me to rid the house of his grandmother's ghost. He expected me to do it for free."

"So you turned him down." I studied him. "Why? I thought you were of the opinion that ghosts didn't belong here in the world of the living."

"You expect too much, girl." He turned away, puffing out smoke. "What's one more ghost in a place like this?"

"Is that why you stopped doing your job?" I asked. "What did Mr Renner say to that, then?"

"He said he didn't need my help," he said. "But if you want to rid yourself of that ghost, I'd suggest you do so before she becomes too strong."

"That was the plan." Assuming Mr Renner let me back into the house after I'd all but accused him of bumping off his own grandmother. If the Reaper wouldn't help, though, who else could? "Is Dolores Malone's ghost around?"

"I expect she is." He backed into the hallway, puffing out a cloud of smoke.

That settled that, then. I turned my back on the Reaper and headed back downhill, towards where Mart waited for me at a safe distance from the Reaper's cottage. If old Dolores's ghost was willing to talk, then I might be able to get the answers I needed after all.

Unfortunately, getting into the retirement home would be tricky even if Mr Renner hadn't told tales on me. I was fresh out of excuses, but there was one person who had the authority to get both of us into there and in front of the person likely to give us answers. If he forgave me, that is.

As I caught up with Mart, he turned to me with his mouth pressed in a scowl. "Much better. I thought I was going to be trapped in that old git's house forever."

"I'm sorry," I said to him. "I—"

"Spare me the apologies," he interrupted. "Look, I know you didn't mean for me to end up stuck with that miserable old man, but really, it wasn't that bad in the end. I think he's lonely."

"He could have sent you to the afterlife, though," I said. "I should have guessed he'd sense you spying on him."

"I can't promise I wasn't a little put out by that," he said. "But you've had a lot on your mind. The evil old ghost. The teenage blogger who's adopted you as a big sister. The detective you'd like to go on a date with."

"Who said anything about going on a date with anyone?" I said. "Did *you* know he was an actual police detective, too? Has everyone here been conspiring in this ridiculous joke?"

"Yeah, we've all been laughing at you," he said. "No, it

was obvious from the moment he showed up in that house."

"I guess I should have known," I allowed. "I've been spending too much time around ghosts. My skills at handling real people are a little rusty."

"I'll pretend that wasn't as insulting as it sounded," he said. "Anyway, I think he should have told you, but he was so fixated on figuring out how to ask you out that he forgot the obvious."

"Mart, please stop commenting on my dating life," I said. "I need to speak to Dolores's ghost."

"Her?" he said. "It might interest you to know that she's been seen in the retirement home. Also, I see your boyfriend over there."

I followed his line of sight and spotted Drew walking across the bridge.

"He's not my boyfriend," I said. "But I reckon I'm going to need the police on my side for this part."

"Ooh, breaking the law again?" He floated behind me. "Do tell."

"Not breaking the law, just doing a little sleuthing," I said. "It's a lot easier when you have the law on your side."

"Especially if 'the law' is as hot as he is," he said.

"Don't be ridiculous." I quickened my pace, and Mart fell back as I caught up with Drew.

The detective came to a halt at the foot of the hill, and disbelief widened his eyes.

"Maura?" he said. "Thank goodness—I thought you'd left town and I was too late."

"For what?" I asked.

"For me to apologise for deceiving you, of course," he

said. "Truth be told, I thought you'd judge me for using your talent to gain information for my own investigation."

I blinked at him. "Seriously? I thought you didn't even believe I could see ghosts."

"I doubted you at first, but Carey's trust of you convinced me to change my mind," he said. "They're a good family. Her and her mum."

"At least we agree on one thing," I murmured. "Look, I realise this is probably the worst time to ask for a favour—"

"What kind of favour?" he asked. "If it's within my power, I'd be glad to help you out."

"I haven't even told you what I need help with yet," I said. "Are the others still at Mrs Renner's house? The construction crew, Mr Renner—everyone except Carey and me?"

"As far as I'm aware, they are," he said. "I briefly checked in, but there's been no progress on the repairs, nor on removing the spell."

"At least they're acknowledging the spell is a problem," I said. "I know I shouldn't have accused Mr Renner like that. I just couldn't think of anyone else who might have been responsible."

Except Dolores, but she'd already paid for her curiosity with her life.

"You came to the logical conclusion, given the evidence," he said. "I was on my way to speak with the Reaper about his clandestine meetings with Mr Renner."

"I already spoke to him," I said. "It sounded like Mr Renner tried to convince him to banish his grandmother's ghost without payment, but the Reaper didn't want to know. Granted, the Reaper is as capable of lying as anyone else."

"I suppose he is," he said. "Were you on your way back to Mrs Renner's house? Is that what you wanted my help with—to speak to Mr Renner?"

"Not him," I said. "I need someone to come with me to the retirement home. Preferably someone with authority, and right now, that's you."

His brows shot up. "Any reason?"

"To speak to a resident," I said. "A dead one, that is. I'm told that Dolores's ghost is there, but I reckon the staff might get suspicious if I show up alone. Still up for helping me out?"

"Of course," he insisted. "I wouldn't mind speaking to her myself, but I lack the necessary skillset."

"Yeah, this isn't really an orthodox way of solving crimes," I said. "My comment about it being standard in magical communities was an exaggeration."

"I thought so," he said. "But that doesn't change the fact that it's a lot easier with someone like you on the team."

A Reaper, or a witch? I managed to shove that question aside before my mouth got me into trouble again. It wouldn't do to expect more of him than he intended to give, and for all I knew, he was just acting out of a misplaced sense of guilt about how he'd researched my history and nearly driven me out of town.

Whether he just felt sorry for me or something else, it didn't matter. Time was running out, but I had someone on my side who could help me get to the truth, one way or another.

14

For our first step, we had to find Dolores Malone's ghost and find out if she knew more about the spell on Mrs Renner's house. It was a long shot, but with none of the current construction workers able to figure out when it had been put there and Mr Renner refusing to cooperate, I could do worse than speak to the one person who'd been around at the time. Even if she was, you know, dead.

Drew and I made straight for the retirement home, and he knocked on the door. Then we waited.

"So," I said, to fill the silence. "Next you're going to tell me you're secretly a Reaper yourself. You never did tell me what type of paranormal you are."

He grinned. "If you guess right, I'll buy you a drink."

My face warmed up, but before I could say more, the door opened, revealing the same goblin as before.

"You again?" Frankie looked from me to Drew. "Are you here on official business? Because we've already answered enough questions, and our residents are getting quite agitated by all the drama."

"Don't worry, we're not here to speak to you," he said. "We're here to speak to Mrs Malone's ghost. Or rather, Maura here is."

"Oh, her," she said, without so much as blinking. "Some of the residents have been talking about seeing her in the garden, but it's hard to say what's real and what's imagined, with some of them. Come on in."

It seemed I'd made the right call when I'd recruited Drew to accompany me to speak to the ghost, because she didn't even ask any questions when we walked through the main room. The other residents looked at me with interested expressions—or, more specifically, at Drew. I heard one of them say, in a carrying whisper, "Has Drew finally got himself a girlfriend?"

"I don't recognise her."

"It's about time, either way."

"I thought he was saving himself for me."

"*Alice.*"

I rolled my eyes, feeling my face heat up, and Drew chuckled under his breath. "It seems your presence has caused a stir."

"Speak for yourself." I'd deal with putting the rumours to rest later. First, I had a ghost to find and a murder to solve.

As I'd hoped, Mrs Malone occupied the same table and chair as beforehand, except she floated instead of sat, her pasty face now transparent. I stopped for an instant, unsure what to say. From her calm manner, Dolores didn't appear the sort of spirit who'd flip out and throw a tantrum when I reminded her that she was dead, but you could never be quite certain.

"Oh, hello," she said, spotting me. "It's you… Maura, was it?"

"Yes, and I think it's my fault you're dead." The words came out in a rush before I could hold them back. I sensed Drew's eyes on me, but he didn't step in to ask what I meant. Or put handcuffs on me, thankfully. Then again, he couldn't see or hear her, only me.

"I beg your pardon?" she said. "You aren't to blame for anything, dear. I'm the one who foolishly decided to try reasoning with Elizabeth Renner. Really, after everything she's done, it was inevitable that she'd have the last word."

A chill raced down my back. "What do you mean by 'everything she's done'?"

"We knew each other since childhood," she said. "The two of us belonged to the same coven. We were rivals from an early age, and she was always jealous that I occupied a higher position in the coven than she did. We engaged in petty pranks… you know the sort. But otherwise, we got along fine. That is, until the floods."

"The floods?" I looked questioningly at Drew. "What floods?"

"A couple of decades ago, the river overflowed," Drew said. "It's the worst tragedy the town has ever faced. Is that what she's talking about?"

"Our entire coven was affected," said the ghost. "Elizabeth's house sat on the river, so she got hit worse than most of us. I tried to persuade her to move in here with me, but she wasn't having any of it. She insisted on staying in that house."

"Even though it was underwater?" I said, nonplussed. "How'd she manage that?"

"She built an extension laced with a shielding spell to keep the water out," she said. "A shoddy job all around, but it worked. She got to keep her house and stayed put."

"So she's been there ever since," I said. "When did Mr Renner come to town? Around the time of the floods?"

"No, he was only a child at the time," she said. "But her memory goes back a long way, and she's always been paranoid that the floods were the work of someone inside her own coven."

"Why would she think the floods were caused by someone in the coven?" I said the last part aloud for Drew's benefit.

Drew cleared his throat. "The floods may have had a magical cause. It's never been proven, and it was long enough ago that a fair portion of the people who might have been able to work out the truth have left town or passed on."

Or not. After all, there are enough ghosts here. I filed that piece of information away for later and got back to the task at hand.

"She was paranoid," Dolores went on. "Refused to re-join the coven even when her money began to dwindle. Of course the house started to fall apart. She always got into fights with anyone she hired to fix the place, so they never finished the job. Finally, a couple of years back, her grandson came to the town."

I leaned forwards. "Mr Renner came here… why?"

"He wanted her to move out of the house and to sell it," she said. "Needless to say, she told him to get stuffed."

"And did he do anything in retaliation?" I asked.

"I wouldn't know."

"The construction workers found a spell had been cast on the house," I explained. "They seemed to think it was put in there when the extension was built, but not who did it. It makes no sense for Mrs Renner to damage her own house."

"Spell?" she said. "Are you sure it isn't just her own spell? She glued that extension on as efficiently as stapling a broomstick back together. It was always going to fall apart."

"Her own spell?" I said. "But… she seemed certain someone else put it there."

"Did she?" said Dolores. "Whatever the case, that place is on its last legs. If I were you, I'd tear the whole house down before someone gets seriously hurt—or worse."

A shiver ran down my back. "You mean like you? Why did you go back to the house the other day?"

"I should have known better than to think I could reason with her," she said. "But I felt I owed it to the rest of my coven to try."

"Okay." I nodded to Drew. "That's all we needed to know."

"Thanks for talking to us," Drew said. "We'll leave now."

"We will," I said. "Um, if you ever feel like moving on, I can arrange it myself if you like. I know the Reaper has no intention of helping any of the ghosts in town, but if you want my help, feel free to ask me anytime."

"That's very generous of you to offer," she said. "I'll be in touch, sweetheart."

At least one ghost was grateful to meet a Reaper. In my experience, older witches and wizards didn't fear what came after death, for the most part. They knew as well as I did that the living were more of a nuisance by far.

I rose to my feet, and Drew and I retraced our steps through the retirement home and to the exit.

"I think she was telling the truth." I waited until the door closed behind us to talk to Drew. "Or what she thought to be the truth, anyway. She said Mrs Renner built the extension herself using magic to protect herself from the floods, then refused to move out. But she's not clear on who bumped her off."

"It fits in with what I know of Mrs Renner's history," he said. "Her grandson, too."

"Wait, so you knew he was after the house?" I said. "Is that why he came to town two years ago?"

"I expect so, but her grandson has every reason to want the house," he said. "For that reason, it makes sense that he wants the ghost gone."

"Question is, did he want the same of the living person?" I asked. "Or was Mrs Renner's shoddy shielding spell the cause of her death, and everything she told me a lie?"

I couldn't discount the possibility. Being dead didn't make her any more truthful than she'd been when she was alive. But if she'd lied, everyone in that house might be in danger.

"Even she lied, there's no guarantee her grandson will listen to reason and cancel the construction work until it's safe," he responded. "He's convinced this should have been a quick and easy job."

"Which is why he tried to make the Reaper get rid of her for free." I gave an eye-roll. "Ghost-hunting might be a dying art, but it's worth paying for."

Despite my light tone, worry gnawed at me. This particular ghost had stuck around far too long already, and Mr Renner hadn't seemed to care how much danger he might be putting everyone in by making them stay in the house.

"I agree," Drew said. "If it helps, I think you can do it. I'll work my powers of persuasion on Mr Renner to get you into the house."

My brow arched. "You seem confident. Sure you aren't hiding a wand up your sleeve?"

"That would be telling." He eyed the inn as we drew closer. "It feels remiss to leave your young friend behind, but I think this is going to be too dangerous for her."

"I have an inkling that if I leave her out of this, she'll end up hiding under a table anyway." I walked towards the inn, trying to quell my misgivings. "Besides, I have a feeling we might need an objective outsider to watch our negotiations."

"If you're sure," he said. "It might be dangerous… is that her mother?"

I halted, spotting Allie. She hurried in our direction until she halted in front of us.

"Maura," said Carey's mother. "Have you seen my daughter?"

"Why, isn't she at home?" My heart gave an uneasy flip.

"She went out not long after Drew dropped her back at home," she said. "Said she was meeting you."

Oh, no. "I went to see the Reaper, and then Dolores's ghost. I haven't seen Carey since I left."

Had she gone back to the house? With the construction crew around, it wasn't as though she'd be alone in there, but that didn't make it any safer.

Her mouth pinched. "I can't leave the restaurant unat-tended, but I'm worried for her."

"I'll find her," I vowed. "Drew and I are going back to Mrs Renner's house. Maybe Carey decided to head back there."

I couldn't think of anywhere else she might be, but knowing what I knew now, I couldn't quell the notion that I'd left it too late.

Drew and I walked at a fast pace, without speaking to one another. I knew he must be thinking the same as I was. While Mr Renner had chased Carey out earlier, her curiosity knew no bounds, and if she'd thought I'd left town and wasn't coming back, then maybe she'd decided to take matters into her own hands. I hoped not, because Mrs Renner's ghost was already too powerful for a regular banishment. And with one Reaper refusing to step in, I was the only person left who might be able to stop her.

Drew slowed as we reached the house. The door and gate were both shut, and nobody stood outside. I didn't hear any voices from the inside, either.

I glanced at Drew. "Did the construction workers go home?"

"I wouldn't have thought Mr Renner would have let them leave without a fuss." He opened the gate and entered the front garden, crouching to pick up the spare key under the doormat. "The key's not here. They must still be inside."

A scream came from inside the house. *Carey.*

"Carey?" I ran up to the door, my heart sinking into my shoes. "Carey, are you in there? Is anyone with you?"

I couldn't hear any voices, but my own heartbeat was

loud enough, and a swamping cold sensation pressed down on me from all angles. It took me a second to recognise the sensation as my long-dormant Reaper senses informing me there was a ghost inside the house.

Bit late there, Reaper senses. I ignored the chill and pushed against the door, but it didn't give. Someone had locked it from the inside. I dug into my pocket and used my wand to cast an unlocking charm, and Drew entered ahead of me.

The hall stood empty, but I heard voices, muted, from somewhere near the back of the house. Drew and I followed the murmur of voices to the kitchen door. I tried the handle, and a shock of cold jolted through my palm.

"Ow!" I let go of the handle. "I wouldn't touch that. Carey, are you in there?"

Drew shoved on the door with his shoulder. "Are you in there? Mr Renner?"

The rumble of muted voices quietened.

"The police are here!" Mr Renner said to someone in the room, his sharp voice impossible to miss. "This blasted ghost locked us in. Let us out."

"Might be tricky," I lifted my wand and cast an unlocking charm, but it wasn't any ordinary lock holding the kitchen door closed. As I'd feared, my spell had no effect, and the door didn't budge an inch. "She's frozen the place up. I guess the Reaper was right when he said she was getting stronger."

Drew's brows rose. "The ghost is holding the door shut? How is that possible?"

"Because she's stronger than before." Strong enough to awaken my Reaper senses for the first time in years.

Carey's scream echoed from above. Drew took a step back. "She's not downstairs. She's above us."

"I'm going up there to get her." I backed away from the kitchen door. "Drew, can you try to get everyone out? If I distract the ghost, I might be able to get her to let go of the door so everyone can escape the house."

"But—" Drew halted, his hand on my arm. I hadn't even noticed he'd moved, but my heart skipped a beat at his touch. "All right. But please don't risk your life any more than you have to."

"Can't make any promises, but we Reapers are pretty resilient."

I backed away, heading for the upper floor. The instant I stepped onto the bottom stair, an invisible force pushed me backwards, and a ferocious breeze struck up, roaring down the stairs and through the hallway.

"Get out!" screamed Mrs Renner.

The whole house trembled with the force of her anger, and I hopped off the stairs before the force caused me to lose my balance. The doors rattled in their frames, but when I peered down the hall to check on Drew, it didn't look like he'd managed to free the others from their room yet.

"How is she so much stronger than before?" Drew leant against the wall, bracing his feet on the floor.

"Because she's drawing on the fear of everyone inside the house," I said grimly. "When ghosts stay on earth beyond their natural span, they generally start to fade away unless they have something particularly strong to anchor them here. Her own anger has been enough to tie her to this house until now, but if she has the others trapped in here, she can draw on their fear for as long as they're within reach of her."

Worse, if she took in more energy than she could expend herself, then there was nowhere for it to go. She might well bring the whole house crashing down... and that was bad news for everyone inside it. Including both of us.

He turned to face me, his eyes rounding. "She's drawing on our fear? All of us?"

"Yeah, but don't ask me how it works. I skipped that part of Reaper training." I put my wand in my pocket and prepared to try the stairs again.

"Does it only work on humans?" asked Drew. "Drawing on our emotions, that is?"

"Uh... why?" I tried to ascend the stairs again, but the same invisible force pushed me backwards into the hall.

"I can think of a way to weaken her." He moved back from the kitchen door... and then he shifted into a giant wolfhound.

My mouth fell open. He was a shifter? "I thought you said no more secrets."

He growled in answer, then bounded towards the locked door and slammed into it. The door trembled, and I suspected even the ghost's power would crumble under the force. His claws dug into the frame and tugged, and a growl slipped from his teeth. The wood splintered and cracked, while the force pushing me downstairs weakened slightly.

Now was my shot. I needed to get to Carey, and it was about time I had some stern words with Mrs Renner.

15

D espite the loud sound of the kitchen door collapsing downstairs, the invisible force continued to push against me as I tried to climb the stairs. I gritted my teeth, shadows flooding out from my body to cover the ground beneath my feet and stop me from losing my balance and falling downstairs.

I'd never had access to the full repertoire of Reaper tricks, but one of the most useful ones was the ability to set foot in places no ordinary person should be able to access. If need be, we could walk through walls or into the ocean to find a soul in need of escorting into the afterlife. An invisible shield conjured by an angry ghost ought to be nothing in comparison.

I climbed the stairs, the shadows bolstering me. Every step was painful, but knowing Carey was trapped upstairs spurred me on, kept me climbing. Five steps to go. Four. Three...

The house gave another tremor, and the stair gave way beneath my foot. I caught my balance against the banister, cursing under my breath. My foot wavered, then I managed to hop over the collapsed stair without falling through.

I could hear the ghost laughing above my head. Then a pair of invisible hands tugged at my ankle, threatening to pull me downstairs.

"Cut it out!" I kicked out, but of course, the ghost was impervious to physical damage.

Shadows flowed around my leg for long enough to detach her grip. I held onto the banister and pulled myself upwards. *I will do this. I will.*

After what felt like an eternity but was probably no more than several seconds, I dragged myself to the top of the stairs and hopped over the hole in the floorboards. Then I faced the darkness ahead of me.

"Carey?" I called out.

"Maura!" Her voice was faint and came from behind the closed door to the master bedroom. I didn't need to try to open it to know the ghost's power held it shut fast.

"Not cool, ghost," I said. "Let her go."

"She had the nerve to try to banish me." Mrs Renner's ghost appeared slowly at first, flickering into existence and hovering above the floor. "Too bad her simple witch tricks are no match for someone as strong as I am."

I was afraid of that. Carey had thought I'd left town, and with the Reaper still refusing to help, she'd decided to try out a banishment of her own. But the ghost had simply been too powerful.

"You've stayed way past your sell-by date," I told her. "You lied to me. More than once. There was no hostile spell used on your house by someone out to harm you. You put a spell on the house yourself to protect it from the floods, then refused to accept anyone else's help or move out when it inevitably started falling apart on you."

She didn't say a word, neither to confirm nor deny my accusations.

"And then you tried to scheme against poor Dolores to stop her from persuading you to move out," I went on. "Your spell backfired, and the house collapsed on your own head. Is that right?"

Mrs Renner gave a sniff. "It's her fault, not mine. She kept trying to convince me to give up the house, as if it was any of her business."

"Forgive me if I don't believe you," I said. "You died by accident, I'll give you that, but then you used your ghostly skills to terrorise everyone who tried to move in. I suppose you wanted to drive away the police at first so they wouldn't find out what you did. That's why you were so set on Detective Drew staying away."

"He should have left me be," she said. "So should you."

"You didn't want him coming here because you knew he'd be persistent enough to figure out the truth," I said. "You were deceiving me from the start. And then to add insult to injury, you killed poor Dolores the way you always planned to when she came here to help you out."

"She came here to *drive* me out," she said. "She truly thought she could persuade me to leave. As though she'd be any more successful when I was dead than when I was alive."

"Then I'll have to do it instead." I looked her in the eyes. "This is your chance to come with me calmly and without further strife. If you want any kind of peace to come of this, I'd suggest you take my advice."

"Never," she snarled. "This is my house. I won't give it

up, not to the police or my ungrateful offspring or anyone else."

The whole house trembled as she spoke. She was more powerful than ever now, drawing on the fear and anger and negative emotions of the others while they'd been trapped inside. If I didn't get her out, and soon, the ripple effects might spread to the neighbouring houses, too. She was far past the point of calming down enough for me to be able to lay her to rest peacefully.

I had to tap into my Reaper skills, because I was all out of other ideas.

"Maura!" Carey yelled from behind the closed door. "Help me!"

The house gave another tremor. I hopped aside as the floorboards shook and splintered, and plaster dust rained down from the ceiling.

"Stop that!" I moved to the door and gave it a shove. The wooden door wouldn't give. *Okay. Time to see if my Reaper skills are up to scratch.*

I let shadows unfold around my hands and feet the same way I had when I'd climbed the stairs. Then I stepped through the shadows—and straight through the door as though it didn't exist.

Carey startled upright when I emerged in the master bedroom. "You… did you just walk through the door? When it was closed?"

"Reaper trick." I crossed the room to her side. Despite her screaming, she looked unhurt, while there wasn't any significant damage to the room. A few herbs lay scattered in heaps around the edges, a constructed spell intended to drive away spirits. It wasn't a bad idea, and if Mrs Renner hadn't been so powerful, it might have worked.

Carey rose to her feet, her goggles bouncing on her head. "How is she so powerful?"

"She knows she's close to the end, and her desperation is making her stronger," I said. "She's getting a boost from our fear, too, so I'm gonna have to ask you to be brave for a moment. Can you do that?"

She gave a frantic nod. I, meanwhile, faced the door, which remained held closed by the invisible force of the ghost's determination.

"There's no point in holding the door shut now," I said to Mrs Renner.

"I beg to differ," her voice came from thin air. "There's no way for you and the girl to both escape this room. She's no Reaper."

My hands fisted. Shadows flowed around me, and I heard Carey exhale in panic. "Show your face, Mrs Renner."

"I won't."

Another blast shook the house, and then a series of crashing noises came from outside. The floor heaved beneath our feet.

This might hurt a little. "Carey, hang onto me!"

She grabbed my arm with a stifled yell—and the floor gave way beneath our feet. At the same time, I conjured as many shadows as I could muster, willing them to break our fall. The shadows masked the house, spread out wider and wider. Surrounding us in a dark mass.

It was too late to turn back. I'd brought Carey with me into the afterworld.

"Carey, hold onto me," I whispered. "Don't look around. Hang on..."

Mrs Renner appeared, a twisted grin on her face—but a hand grabbed hers before she could reach for Carey.

Dolores Malone's ghost appeared, holding Mrs Renner's hand in her grip. "That's enough, Elizabeth."

"You again?" said Mrs Renner. "Couldn't you leave me be? Don't tell me you still want my house even now."

"Nobody wants your house, you twisted, evil old woman," said Dolores. "I won't let you hurt any more innocent people."

Mrs Renner's eyes narrowed, her grey hair blew around her transparent face, and fury radiated outwards from her body. "I will not die!"

Conscious of Carey clinging to my back, I focused hard, crossing my fingers that the afterworld would still recognise me as a Reaper. After a short, painful pause, a door appeared among the shadows. Tall, glowing around the edges, and suspended in mid-air. Mrs Renner spotted it and broke from Dolores's grip with a furious yell.

"I will not leave!" Her ice-cold arm gripped mine. "And if I must, I'm taking you with me."

"Let go of my sister!" Mart collided with her from the side, knocking her grip loose.

As Carey cowered behind me, I caught Mrs Renner's hand in my own, and held fast. "You're coming with me."

Mrs Renner flailed, kicking and screaming, but the door opened at my command, revealing a yawning chasm of absolute blackness. Even on the brink, she fought me. Weaker this time, as though she'd used up most of her strength. She gave one last desperate tug, then I let go, pushing her over the door's threshold and into the true afterlife.

The yawning blackness swallowed her, and then blessed silence descended in her wake.

Dolores hovered at my side. "Is she gone?"

"I hope so." I turned to her. "And you?"

She floated forwards, a dreamy expression on her face. "Yes… yes, I think it's time. Thank you, Maura."

The current of air from the open door caught her, and she passed through it into nothingness.

I turned to Mart next, my heart in my throat. "You…"

"Don't even think about it." He wrapped both ice-cold arms around me, solid in a way he couldn't be in the waking world. "I'm going nowhere, Reaper Witch. Now close that door before something nasty gets out."

The shadows folded back, and the door closed at my command. I released a slow breath, letting go of Mart. Carey stared open-mouthed at him. Here in the after-world, nothing was hidden.

"This is Mart," I told her. "My twin brother."

"Oh," she said, looking slightly dazed. "Hey, Mart."

"Nice to meet you." He jerked his head at me. "Go on, get us out of here."

"You can fly," I pointed out. "Carey, hang onto me. I'll get us both out."

She held onto my hand as I walked through the shadows, my brother floating at my side. A glance confirmed the stairs were still intact beneath me, but I didn't dare let the shadows drop until we stood on solid ground. Then the shadows folded outwards, revealing the ruins of the collapsed house around us. The construction crew filled the back garden, along with Mr Renner… and Drew, back in his human form again.

Carey shifted at my side. "I don't think my camera recorded all that."

"I hope it didn't, otherwise the Reaper Council might have the two of us arrested." I tried for a jokey tone, but it didn't really work, considering the chaos surrounding us. "C'mon, let's get out."

As we were picking our way through the ruins, Drew noticed me first, striding towards the house. "Maura! You're alive. I thought—"

"It's over," I said. "She's gone. Into the afterworld."

Only now did I realise I was shaking. I hadn't banished any souls in months, and now I'd used my powers twice in a day. I really needed a nap, but it seemed I wouldn't get one. Drew and the others descended on the pair of us, along with a sizeable crowd who must have been drawn by the noise of the collapsing house. Questions bounced off me like pebbles, none of which I could answer.

I like to think Drew was the one who caught me when I passed out, but I think the shadows got me first.

16

"Hey, some of the footage came out okay," Carey said to me. The two of us sat at a table together in the restaurant, my laptop open on the desk. I'd loaned it to her to help her extract the useful bits of the footage from Mrs Renner's house, since the couple of computers here at the inn were out of date and didn't have the right software.

Since both Carey and I had been stuck indoors since our close call at Mrs Renner's house, we'd spent the last few days going through the recordings and the footage Carey had captured of the ghost. It would still take a lot of editing work to get it into good shape for her to upload, but it gave her something to do while she was grounded.

I wasn't technically grounded myself, of course, but I'd been paid on the condition that I didn't drag Carey into any more scrapes. I was more than happy to stay out of trouble for the foreseeable future. At least until Mr Renner packed his bags and left, which seemed a long way off. Things were tense between him and Carey's mother—

who'd found out about his insulting comments towards her daughter—but since his grandmother's house was in pieces, he didn't have much choice but to stay here at the inn until everything was finalised.

Not that I in any way regretted helping her move into the next world. With any luck, she and Dolores would both be at peace now.

"I doubt Mr Renner will want to be included in the footage." I pointed to the screen. "Um, also, Drew doesn't want the whole universe to know he's a shifter."

She giggled. "Everyone knows, though. Everyone in town, anyway."

I rolled my eyes. I hadn't seen the detective since he'd been forced to step in to deal with the aftermath of Mr Renner losing his inheritance in the house's collapse and to stop him from taking out his anger on the construction workers. I'd been hoping to see him, if just to clear up any loose ends, but I'd been happy enough helping Carey write her blog account of our misadventures—with the names changed, of course.

"That bit works." I pointed out a section of footage of the house shaking under Mrs Renner's assault. "Though if you're going to keep picking such dangerous places to go ghost-hunting, maybe you should invest in some more equipment. Like a safety helmet."

Allie cleared her throat behind me. "Carey is going to take some time off ghost-hunting for a while. She's missed enough school already."

"I haven't had enough," she insisted. "This was a special case. I want to keep blogging. I've already got two extra subscribers, look."

"I think Drew is one of them," her mother said.

"Don't spoil it," she said.

He's been reading Carey's blog, but he hasn't stopped by to talk to me? I shoved the thought aside. He didn't owe me an audience, and besides, he was busy.

Still. I wanted to see him before I left town… which would happen as soon as I had the heart to leave Carey behind. Or her mother kicked me out of the inn. One or the other.

Allie turned to me. "Maura, can I talk to you?"

Oh. I guess this is it. My heart gave an uneasy drop, and I rose to my feet, trying to hide the panic from my expression. "Sure. I'll be back in a second, Carey."

Bracing myself, I left the restaurant and walked with Allie through the glass doors connecting it with the inn's lobby. "I don't think I ever properly thanked you. For saving my daughter's life."

"Oh." I felt myself flushing. "Honestly, I'm just glad I could help her."

"Yes, it's good that she finally has a friend." She shook her head. "She's had a difficult few years, and while I'd berate her for taking risks, this is the most adventurous she's been in a long time."

I fidgeted, unsure what she was getting at. "I feel like I've overstayed my welcome. I thought it would be a quick job. Getting rid of the ghost, I mean."

"Don't worry about it," she said. "You did a really good job helping out at reception the other day, too."

"Honestly, it was no big deal. And it's the least I could have done to repay you for the trouble I've caused you."

"Don't be ridiculous." She extended a hand, holding out a handful of twenty-pound notes. "This is for the shift you worked, on top of the payment for banishing the ghost."

"But—" I protested.

"You saved my daughter's life." She pushed the money into my hand. "And you helped the town deal with a dangerous spirit. You're welcome to stay here at the inn for as long as you like. I understand you have another home… or do you?"

"I have an apartment." With this payment, I could afford another month's rent, but without a secure job, I might well end up in the same position again within a few weeks. "But I'm only there for a short while. Then I have to figure out my plan."

She nodded. "Well, if you want to take on any shifts here at the inn, you're more than welcome to. We've had the need for more staff for some time, but we haven't been able to find anyone willing to make the commitment."

"All right. If you need me to do any more shifts, let me know." I pocketed the money. "I've already stayed longer than I planned."

She smiled. "We don't get many new people in town, but I think you're going to be a good influence."

"I agree," said a deep male voice.

I nearly jumped out of my skin. Drew had appeared behind her, in a stealthy way which I suspected had to do with him being a shifter.

"Whoa." I held a hand to my racing heart. "Don't make me jump like that."

Laughter sounded from behind me, and Mart grinned across the lobby. I studiously ignored him.

"I apologise," said Drew. "Can we talk? If you aren't busy."

"She isn't, yet," said Allie, and winked at me.

Honestly. Anyone would think she'd been talking to my brother.

Mart's laughter pursued me as I walked outside with Drew. I could sense him watching me, but I had no idea what was going through his head. Nor was I quite sure what to ask first. "Have you finished dealing with Mr Renner?"

"Almost," he said. "I expect he'll leave town within the next day. Which is both good news and bad news, because the town needs the business."

No wonder Allie had been able to give me such a high payment. "I think the construction team will be glad to be rid of him."

"I agree," he said. "There's nothing left of the house to sell, so he tried to blame it on the witch coven his mother belonged to. Since multiple eyewitnesses saw that his own grandmother demolished the house, though, the coven leader was able to overrule him."

"Good," I said. "With that many witnesses, he had some cheek trying to blame anyone other than the ghost for knocking the place down. I know most of them couldn't see her ghost, but still."

"Yes, and she was a murderer to boot." He grimaced with distaste. "I had to explain to the staff at the retirement home, which should be some relief to poor Dolores's family."

"She helped me get rid of Mrs Renner's ghost in the end," I said. "I saw her off."

"I thought it was something like that." He eyed me.

"You didn't suffer any lasting damage? I worried when you collapsed on me."

So it had been him who'd caught me after all? Under his gaze, my face heated. "Nah, I guess I was just out of practise using my Reaper skills. And that ghost was a strong one."

We came within sight of Mrs Renner's house—or what was left of it. The remains of the manor house had already been cleared away, leaving nothing but an empty space behind.

"The construction crew removed the rubble," he said. "Mr Renner took most of the furniture that survived in one piece, and that was that."

I scanned the empty space. "No more ghosts, either."

Not that the town was in any way a ghost-free zone, but it surprised me how readily I'd grown used to seeing transparent figures on the streets. While they sometimes gave me curious glances, I'd learned my lesson about using warmth spells in public, and now they mostly left me alone.

"I'll have to take your word for it on that," said Drew. "Mr Renner gave the land back to the coven so they can build something else there. I get the impression he wanted to leave town as quickly as possible after his appeal failed."

"Good," I said. "It's not like he can blame anyone living for the state of the house, though it shouldn't surprise me that he tried."

Drew turned away from the manor house. I was suddenly conscious of how close he was, and my mind went blank for a moment before the obvious question came to mind.

"So," I said. "A shifter? Really?"

"I'd have thought you'd have guessed," he said.

"I didn't peg you for a wizard, but I've never met any shifters who work as detectives before." I grinned.

"I'm surprised you haven't," he said. "We have excellent tracking skills."

I tilted my head. "Go on, tell me what else you've been hiding. It's only fair. You know everything about me."

"I don't know everything about you," he said. "I don't know, for instance, if you're going to be staying in town for much longer."

"I'm fairly sure Carey's mother was in the middle of offering me a full-time position at the inn when you showed up."

His brow rose. "In what capacity?"

"Either at the inn or the restaurant," I said. "I'm still working on long-term plans, as you may have gathered."

"Like ghost-hunting?" he said. "You have a good track record. Like you said."

"See what I mean?" I gave him an eye-roll. "You read my entire history."

"Only the information that was available on the web within the magical world, which isn't as much as I'd have preferred," he said. "Have you been living in non-magical towns since you left your coven?"

"Mostly," I said. "I'm not always a ghost hunter. Not supposed to be, anyway. But if I stay here..."

Two ghosts drifted past. I followed them with my gaze, and Drew did, too, as though he knew I was looking at something he couldn't see himself.

"If you stay here, you might be obligated to spend

more time with ghosts than you would in other places," he said. "Have you spoken to the Reaper recently?"

"Not since before I went back to Mrs Renner's place," I said. "After I confirmed he and Mr Renner weren't scheming against me. I'm not all that keen to see him again."

"Any reason?"

I glanced around, spotting Mart's ghost hovering nearby. He shrugged and made kissy faces when he saw me looking.

I raised my voice. "Aside from the obvious? Yes. He and I had an argument about my twin brother."

Drew frowned. "Your twin brother? The one who…?"

"Died. Yes." I jabbed a finger directly at Mart, my heartbeat quickening. "He's over there. Let's just say I'm rarely alone, even when I seem to be. Fair warning."

Drew followed my gaze, and Mart did a ridiculous dance which the detective entirely missed. "His ghost follows you around?"

"You've got it," I said. "Which doesn't make me very popular with most Reapers. We're supposed to lay the dead to rest, not bind them to ourselves. But Mart wants to stay, and who am I to say no?"

His expression cleared, as though I'd answered a question he'd been pondering. "So he's your source of information on ghosts?"

"Occasionally," I said. "He's also the reason I can say definitively that any of the reports you might have read on me being responsible for his death are complete nonsense."

His mouth parted. "The reports I've read don't blame you at all. And nor do I."

I looked away, my eyes stinging. Even though I'd come to terms with knowing he knew my past, conversations like this were difficult. Always had been.

"I know some of the coven members blamed me for his death," I murmured, unable to meet his eyes directly. "That's why I couldn't stay. Things are… difficult, with the rest of my family. The witch side, anyway."

"And… the Reaper side?" he asked. "Not my place to judge, but the one thing I know from talking to Harold is that it's generally frowned upon for a Reaper to have a relationship with a human."

"Believe me, I'm not conventional and neither is my family," I said. "I know that much. I also know a career in Reaping is pretty much everything or nothing. Which is why it's not for me."

Neither was belonging to a coven, when it came down to it. Not my birth coven, anyway.

But for now? I had a potential new job. I had a place to stay, and I was well on the way to figuring out a way forward rather than treading water for the first time in my life.

"Just kiss him already!" Mart yelled. "Before His Deathliness gets here."

"Who…?" I looked up, and Drew said, "Speak of the devil."

The Reaper of all people was walking down the road towards me. While I expected him to accost Drew, he halted in front of me instead.

"I need to talk to you," he said brusquely. "Alone."

"I won't be far away." Drew's hand briefly brushed my arm, then he retreated to let the Reaper and I talk in peace.

"Boo!" Mart yelled. The Reaper shot him a glare, and he wilted on the spot.

I stepped between them in case the Reaper decided to get out his scythe after all, but he turned his attention back to me. "You're staying in town."

"For now," I said. "But I'm working at the inn with Carey and her mother. Not as a Reaper. Or a ghost hunter, either."

I'd expected him to be displeased with my answer, and sure enough, he scowled. "There's no opting out without consequences. If you're here, others will follow."

"I did tell you I wasn't going to contact the council, didn't I?" I said. "I won't risk them penalising me for what I did to keep Mart here with me, and besides, I'm not interested in ending up on their radar again."

He shook his head. "That may be, but your presence will stir up questions."

"Like why there's no Reaper," I said. "And why the town is the way it is."

He grunted. "You want the story? You can ask anyone else."

"I don't think so." I looked him in his startlingly blue eyes—his only visible Reaper trait. "You stopped doing your job, and I'd like to know why. I think you owe me the answer."

He was silent for a moment. Then he spoke. "There was a terrible flood in this town nearly two decades ago. The river overflowed, and the whole town was practically underwater. It happened overnight with nowhere near enough warning, so we couldn't evacuate."

"I heard," I said. "I heard that was where Elizabeth

Renner and Dolores Malone's animosity started, as her house was flooded."

"Everyone was affected," he said, his voice a low growl. "You can't even imagine what it would have been like being a Reaper in the middle of a disaster like that. There was no reprieve. No chance to recover. My apprentice and I were worked to the bone. I had to send him out alone more often than I'd have liked. Then he…" He paused. I was silent for a moment, giving him the chance to gather his words.

"My apprentice was one of many who were killed in the aftermath," he finally said. "It shouldn't have happened. You should know we're normally immune to most things which would kill an ordinary person, but the sheer number of souls… it was overwhelming. After that, there were no more Reapers. And the idea of getting all the spirits of those killed and rounding them up… it was too much for me to handle alone."

"I understand."

He didn't say anything else. Nor did he need to. While most people hadn't mentioned the subject aside from Dolores's ghost, I didn't blame the others for not wanting to revisit that painful part of their history.

"As for why I was meeting with Mr Renner," he added, "his family was affected by the floods, too. He came back here initially with his parents, who owned property here. Including… that house."

"But his grandmother didn't want to leave," I said. "So he left and decided to come back later after she died."

I'd figured that much out.

He grunted. "Fools, both of them. Word of advice—stay away from the dead in future."

"Only if they stay away from me."

Which was debatable. Looking at Mart, who was hovering behind the detective making rabbit ears above his head with his ghostly hands, I couldn't foresee myself turning my back on the Reapers entirely.

Regardless, it had been a long while since I'd looked forward to tomorrow with an open mind. Ghosts or no ghosts, I was ready to see what Hawkwood Hollow had to offer.

After years of drifting, it was about time for me to start living again.

ABOUT THE AUTHOR

Elle Adams lives in the middle of England, where she spends most of her time reading an ever-growing mountain of books, planning her next adventure, or writing. Elle's books are humorous mysteries with a paranormal twist, packed with magical mayhem.

She also writes urban and contemporary fantasy novels as Emma L. Adams.

Find out more about Elle's books at: https://www.elleadamsauthor.com/

Find Elle on Facebook at https://www.facebook.com/pg/ElleAdamsAuthor/